PUSHING BACK THE
DARKNESS

PUBLISHED BY
OUR WRITTEN LIVES OF HOPE, LLC

Our Written Lives of Hope provides publishing services for authors in various educational, religious, and human service organizations. For information, visit www.OurWrittenLives.com.

Copyright ©2017 Laura Aranda
Cover photos by David Lisenby
Cover Models: Fayth McCoy and Elizabeth Hughes
Interior Design by Our Written Lives

Library of Congress Cataloging-in-Publication Data
Aranda, Laura 1984
Pushing Back the Darkness

Library of Congress Control Number: 2017903737
ISBN: 978-1-942923-25-1 (paperback)

Scriptures are from various Bible versions, as cited in the text.

PUSHING BACK THE
DARKNESS

LAURA ARANDA

DEDICATION

To all who desire to embody Christ's compassion.
May we all do our part to *Push Back the Darkness.*

FOREWORD

Only God can take a casual Facebook email question about multi-level marketing, and within a couple of years turn it into a friendship with a partner in ministry. That is how I first met Laura Aranda and what a blessing it has been!

As honored as I am to be writing this foreword, I'm equally thrilled to see the subject matter she is tackling in this novel, human trafficking. Personally, when I realized how horrible and widespread modern slavery is, I began to ask, "What can I do to help end it?"

Laura did the same.

She saw a need and found a way to get involved. She jumped headfirst into standing up against human trafficking, and brought as many people—friends, family, and church members—with her as possible. If you have a pulse and the breath of life in your lungs, Laura wants to motivate you to get involved in ending human trafficking and helping the poor.

She has taken her passion for reaching the "least of these," and put it into the story you are about to dig into. In the coming pages, she brings the Gospel of Jesus Christ and the Great Commission into real life situations.

Prepare to be challenged. Prepare to be encouraged. Prepare to change and to become a change agent in our world.

I think that is a great way to describe Laura, an agent of change. Laura, thank you for letting God use you and for showing us how to love God and love our neighbors!

PASTOR BOBBY DANIEL
First Baptist Church of Vinton, Louisiana

Habakkuk 2:2

And the Lord answered me, and said, "Write the vision."

CHAPTER 1

"There are things we don't want to do. Journeys we wish not to take. But our dreams do not care about our ease and comfort. They demand more of us than we are currently capable of, and for that, let us be thankful for them."

— Brendon Burchard

It was the same dream over and over again. The slick laughter played like background music to the midnight terror. A demonic presence loomed over the terrified girl in the cold bed, her frightened face wrenched as always. Her fingers clenched the filthy bed covers as she tried to peer out the dirty window onto the city street.

Claire had seen her before.

The girl always sat straight up in the bed. Mousy-brown hair streamed down her bare shoulders as a tattered muslin blanket covered her from the waist down. The girl screamed, but the dreamer heard no sound.

What was separating them? Was it years? Distance? The girl seemed so close. Claire felt as if she were only feet away, staring into the room from just outside the window.

"She's real. I know she's real," Claire murmured as she tossed and turned.

Somewhere in the night, in a room far away, the girl was trapped. Claire could feel it. The girl was there, steadily waiting for her abuser, or her savior, to arrive.

Something was different this time. The girl tried to move. She was not just silently screaming as she stared into the dark room. She was trying to get up and escape, but her wrists were bound. Handcuffs encircled each one, holding her to the bed. She was a prisoner.

"If I just crack open my eyes, and do not move, not even to peel my cracked lips apart, the nightmare will subside," Claire thought to herself as she struggled to regain consciousness. *"I can lay here. The sweat will dry. My heartbeat will return to a normal pace. The shadow's talons will wither and withdraw. It is sleep paralysis. That is all."*

Claire began to speak to the little girl inside of herself, the one living in the corners of her heart and head, the one who was still afraid.

"Shh. Shh. Just be still. Be still. Wait. Just wait and see. Hear the car horns? Listen. Just listen to the outside world coming and going. It is alright," she said, trying to nurture her inner-child into a peaceful state. Then she started to wake up and began reprimanding herself.

"C'mon! C'mon, now. You are a woman. Not a child. Nothing is going to get you! It is okay. Get up. Breathe. Open your eyes. NOW! There is nothing there. Nothing. That is the rocking chair. Daria's chair. Those are your work clothes hanging over the back of the chair. You have to be in court in the morning. There is your cheval mirror standing behind the chair. There are no monsters, at least none in your house."

Claire Sullivan tentatively sat up in bed. The streetlights outside her bedroom window cast a patch of golden light across the carpeted floor. She could hear a distant siren. Her English bulldog, Maesters, lay plopped on the floor, sound asleep.

If there were any spirits lingering in her room, or nightmares eating away at her imagination, Maesters had no clue of them and no reason to guard her. He had no reason to sound a growling alarm. Padding across the dark bedroom, Claire made her way to flick on the hallway light before venturing to the kitchen.

"Maybe some chamomile tea will help," she said as she rummaged through her collection of loose-leaf herbal teas.

Pictures on the fireplace mantle in the living room caught her attention as she paced her apartment waiting for the teakettle to heat up. She smiled at an old photo of her father laughing as he built a sandcastle on Galveston Beach with her. Judge Patrick Sullivan was once larger than life itself. He made Claire's world spin into motion and revolve around the sun.

Claire made him smile and laugh. She would do anything to take away the weary sadness that constantly tugged at the corners of his lips. It was the memories of her mother that carved out the tired lines across his face.

Claire gazed at the fading photo she kept of her mother, Eva Sullivan. Looking at her was like looking at a reflection in the mirror. Anger bubbled up inside her chest, just as it did when she was a young child, as she thought of how her mom left them. It was unintentional of course, but Mother never was a fighter.

She always gave up at the first sign of resistance. She gave up, even before the word "cancer" passed through the doctor's lips, and never grasped for hope. There was no faith, not a prayer for deliverance, no holding onto life, not even for her daughter's sake. Eva believed her Sully would have everything under control, just as he always did.

Claire remembered herself as a nine-year-old, wanting to pound her mother's frail chest and beg her to fight.

"Please! Just fight! Just once! Just this time. Fight! Why won't you at least try? Why are you giving in? You never even tried!" she thought.

Bitterness tasted like their neighbor's generosity and the week old tuna casseroles Claire and her father ate the week her mother died. Cold resentment glazed over her heart, like grease in the leftover baked chicken dish someone had dropped by that fateful day.

Sipping on her hot tea, Claire came back to the reality of the present moment. Just as quickly as she looked at the empty fireplace, her old memories took her to a different place in time once more.

"All noble things are difficult," he had said.

She could hear his voice echoing in her apartment. Judge Patrick Sullivan uttered Oswald Chamber's words to her, his only child, as he left her apartment fourteen years ago. He saw great potential in Claire. Claire was no exception. He wanted her to become an attorney, to follow in his footsteps of justice.

At age nineteen, Claire had pouted after the argument with her father. At the time, she embodied more of Eva than she could admit. Sometimes, she did not want to do the hard, noble things. She was not enjoying her first year of law school. There was no way she could have foreseen that those words would be the final molding strokes of motivation she would ever receive from her father.

With a sigh, she shook her head and set the cooling tea down on the mantle next to all the pictures.

"This is not helping," she said to herself. A walk down memory's lane was not going to put her back to sleep. Regardless, work would come early in the morning. A few sleeping pills would do the trick. Perhaps they would draw her into a dreamless oblivion, where no memories or nightmares could bite.

Chapter 2

"Why is the human race incapable of using its
power to alleviate suffering?"

—Lydia Cacho

His gentle wisdom and kindness was Christ-like.

Vicious tears burned her eyes and blurred her vision as she re-read the words engraved on her father's marble tombstone.

She could taste blood coming from her tongue as she held back the waves of grief that threatened to geyser like a spire from the well of her soul. She felt muted and colorless. Fourteen years after his murder, Claire could still see his kind, gray eyes filled with wistful hope and a little disappointment the day he left her apartment.

"Daddy! Daddy! Look! Now, do you see? I did it. You would be so proud of me," she said as she reached out and touched the cold slab marker. "If only you could see me now. I am what you always wanted me to be. Aren't I?"

Claire had finished law school and went on to work for Child Protective Services as an administrative lawyer. She was part of the team responsible for analyzing state laws and making recommendations to legislators. The goal closest to her heart was to improve laws to protect children from exploitation. Claire felt like it was her responsibility to be a voice for the voiceless.

As she knelt before her parents' mausoleum, Claire took a deep breath. The morning dew had started seeping through the knees of her pantsuit. All of Houston continued to rush by, unaware that her world had stopped turning.

She was deep enough into the cemetery that she barely heard the traffic noise. The still place had sounds of its own, which Claire recognized from her hours of reminiscing there. The stillness had a movement unknown to most people. It glided over Claire, giving her chills.

October painted a lonely lavender sunrise as the fangs of Houston's scorching summer loosened. A teasing breeze swept tendrils of black hair around Claire's strong, square face. The air played a melody, like the soft sound of glass flutes rising up to the heavens above. She loved this time of year, but the anniversary of her father's unsolved murder would always stain the face of fall.

Though she was over thirty now, the pain of losing her Hercules still crippled her. She prayed that whoever committed the crime would be brought to justice. It was the only way she would allow her soul to find rest.

Her determination brought a sense of condemnation into her heart. How could she believe in an unseen God? How could she even hope to rely on Someone who had disappointed her so much? The rational part of her mind held no debate; she knew she was angry with God.

Her father's funeral was the last time she ever stepped into the old Pasadena church. Though she often whispered prayers, she avoided being real with God and telling Him how she felt. So much time had slipped by since she felt the need to be in God's presence at a church service somewhere.

There was no doubt in her mind about theology. She knew whole-heartedly that there was a God, One God, who robed himself in flesh, came, died for her sins, and rose again. She just did not have anything to say to him. Not now, not anytime soon.

How could Jesus Christ allow such a noble soul to be murdered? A man who did so much for God's Kingdom on Earth? Judge Sullivan was a righteous man, a just, fair judge who would send people to church, counseling, or rehab instead of prison.

The tinkling of Claire's phone tugged her back into her present world of errands, responsibilities, and masks. There were always masks, the facades of happiness, the veil indicating she was fine and nothing was wrong.

"Hello?" Claire answered as she stood and brushed the random blades of grass off her suit.

"Hey, Claire. How are you?" The warm tenor voice of her longtime boyfriend, Cole Peretti made her smile.

"I'm doing better hearing from you." Claire wiped away stray tears, then reached into her purse to fish out her keys.

There was so much between where she was now and where she wanted to be in life. Claire knew what she wanted to be like, but all the ins and outs of the tangled path along the way had changed her. She didn't know who she was anymore.

From the horizon of the present, she could see herself and Cole Peretti in the next phase of life. They were very much happy, very much married. But for now, a weaving precipice of uncertainty loomed, inviting her into the labyrinth of her day.

"Where are you?" Cole asked.

Claire could hear the squad room muted in the background. She responded with awkward silence.

"Ah, I see. You're at the cemetery," he said. He knew her well.

"Lucky guess," Claire replied softly. "But, yes. I just needed to be near them today."

"Rough morning, Sweetheart?"

"Yes. Rough night. I am having those dreams again."

"I'm sorry. Why don't we go out this evening after work? Meet me at Rica's tonight when I get off. I want to see you. Say, six?" Cole asked.

"That sounds perfect. I'm headed to the office now, Love. I will see you tonight," Claire responded with a deep breath. Maybe a night out would take her mind off her disjointed emotions.

"I love you, Claire. See you tonight."

"Until then." Claire started the short hike back to her old Fiat.

"Cole Peretti. Now that's a name I can fall in love with," she thought.

She was eighteen when they met as Bible quizzers. Cole was from Austin. He came with his Bible quiz team to the Houston area for a match in the District Finals.

Cole Peretti. It was a name worth scribbling on notebooks, or in Claire's case, quiz cards. Regardless, that was what teenage love was made of—scribbled ink. They hit it off quite well, even though Cole skunked her one hundred thirty points to sixty-five.

It had been a long fifteen years. So much had changed in both of their lives. Both hearts had somehow sadly hardened.

"Let us just make it through," Claire whispered her desperate plea.

It was her only prayer, one she said over and over again. An almost cynical laugh erupted out of her as she turned one last time to say goodbye to her parents' mausoleum.

That was her prayer? That was all she could come up with to say to God? Then so be it.

The day at the office seemed to last forever, but Claire was finally headed toward Rica's.

"There's never enough parking," she chuntered as she eased the Fiat out of Rica's over-packed parking lot. Glancing at the phone lying on the seat next to her, she sighed with relief.

Cole said he would meet her at six. She had ten minutes to drive around the corner, find a spot to park, and walk in. Cole was not the most punctual person, so she had a little breathing room. A swift sprint back to Rica's would not hurt her any.

The curbside parking along Hawthorne and Wertheimer was taken. Claire was relieved to find a laundromat on Lovett Street with no signs saying that parking was only for customers. Murmuring a swift prayer that her car would not be broken into, she locked the doors and started back up the two blocks to the elixir lounge.

Rica's was a favorite hot spot for locals, but occasionally their events drew people from Dallas and even Louisiana. Area beat-poets and musicians often performed there on open mic night. Thursday was jazz night, and Saturday was for salsa dancing. Rica's hosted annual silent auctions featuring local art and photography; the money went back to help the community.

Memories of dancing the night away in Cole's arms filled Claire's giddy head as she dashed along the narrow sidewalk lined with a tall black fence. She could see the lights and hear the tinkling of laughter just ahead when without warning a vicious dog slammed into the other side of the fence.

Claire increased her speed to move away from the snarls. Her heart had not stopped galloping when a hoarse voice called out from the darkness on the other side of the sidewalk.

"Change for a drink, miss? Any change?"

Panhandlers—or bums as Cole so adeptly labeled them—were unquestionably common in Houston, especially downtown. The man's salt and pepper hair was curly and unkempt. His swarthy skin blended into dusk's gathering darkness, which swallowed him.

Claire's heart tugged her to a stop as the man's dirty, ragged nails reached toward her. He was hungry, yearning, searching.

Where had he come from? Did he have a family? Any kinfolk at all? How did he end up begging? A wet cough vented from his lungs. He was sick.

"Where did you sleep last night?" Claire asked gently as she kneeled beside the man.

He avoided her eyes, unsure why the nicely-dressed woman was kneeling so close to him. "I'm hungry, thirsty," the man said.

"What's your name? Do you have a place to go?"

"I slept out by the greyhound bus stop last night. Name's Dan."

Claire slipped her hand into her purse, pulled out the granola bar she did not eat for breakfast, and pressed it into Dan's rough, dry hands.

"Here, Dan. It's not much, but . . ."

"Claire! There you are! C'mon, quick." Cole Peretti's dark, rich voice jolted Claire's attention away from the homeless man. "I think there may be room on a couch. Quick, or we'll be stuck standing again tonight!"

The sound of Cole's staccato footsteps marched Claire back into the moment, and with a regretful, quick look at the sick beggar, Claire was on her way. It was difficult for her to push him completely out of her mind as the chilly October wind rumpled the edges of her blouse. She dashed the last few yards into Cole's waiting arms.

"Hi. How are you, Sweetheart?" Cole asked as he embraced her in a warm, tight squeeze. "Oh, my goodness! I've missed you." His hug was secure and long. "I'm so tired."

Claire felt good to be back in Cole's strong arms. "I'm good! It's so good to see you. How's the case going?"

"It is going well, Sweetheart, but I'm not asking about any of your cases, or about Josie, so you don't ask about my work. Deal?" Silencing her with a quick kiss, he opened the door to the lounge and ushered her inside. "We can talk about all that later. Let's just allow our brains to come back alive for a while."

"Deal." Claire eagerly squeezed his hand as Cole led the way through the dimly-lit bar to order their usual drinks. The cello, saxophone, and other instruments in the background created a cozy and warm atmosphere as Claire stared at Cole, but not even her favorite local beats could keep her mind in one place tonight.

She smiled as she thought about Josie, the young girl Cole and Claire helped place in her best friend Misti Jacob's home. Sweet memories teased at Claire when she thought of how Josie whispered questions about Cole that first time she met him.

"Is that Benjamin Bratt from Law and Order?"

"No, but almost," Claire had said with a laugh.

Claire gazed at her handsome Italian.

"Cole is perfect in every way, from his perfect height of exactly six-feet, to the way he does his police work, from the way he grills a steak, to the way he melts my heart with his left-dimpled smile. The way . . ."

She could go on, but Claire's attention was torn from her delicious thoughts as a slowly rambling shadow directed her eyes to Rica's front window. It was the beggar, Dan. His ragged pants' hem was inches too short. His cracked and dry heels stuck out from mismatch clogs. A plastic bag hung limply from his arm.

The saxophone and cello had started a new piece when Cole caught Claire gazing at the homeless man. "My work is never done." He cursed as he set his drink down at the bar, and his hand went to his Taser.

"I'll be right back. Let me shoo him off the property, away from the cars." Cole kissed her forehead absently and shouldered his way toward to the door.

Knowing she would never be able to enjoy the jazz, or the watered-down mint julep, Claire followed Cole out into the night.

"Cole! Just leave him. C'mon. You're off work. Let's just head back to my place."

Nodding in disgust, Cole turned and smiled as the shadows dropped from his face. His anger seemed so close to the surface these days, Claire thought.

"Where did you park? I got Joels to drop me off."

Claire looped her arm through Cole's and headed back toward the Fiat. Her mind was as unsettled as the dry, crusty leaves skirting along the pathway.

CHAPTER 3

"Non nobis solum nati sumus.
(Not for ourselves alone are we born.)
Your deeds are your monuments."

—R.J. Palacio

Maesters lay snoring away on Claire's gingham rug at the foot of the wood-planked platform bed she slept on. A shrill ringtone startled them both awake before the sun yawned its warm morning greeting.

Claire sat up, reluctantly reached for her cell, and grumbled a groggy, "Hello."

"Hey there, Sunshine!" A sarcastic female voice replied loudly.

"You're too cheerful in the morning. What time is it anyways?"

"Close to nine, Dear. Josie wants to talk to you."

Misti Jacobs was always up early, even on the weekends. Between morning sprints with her husband Richard and making sure her juice bar, Liquid Life, was open for customers, it was practically noon to Misti.

"Sure, Misti. I'll be right over." Claire mentally mapped out the quickest route to Misti's via Starbucks. Misti might be a juice junkie now, but espresso was still on the top of Claire's food pyramid.

The two women were best friends. They had seen each other at their best—full of life, love, and blossoming careers. They had been there for each other at their worst—in the midst of death, devastation, and brokenness.

Misti had survived two miscarriages, and a birthing a gorgeous stillborn daughter. After that, Misti stayed in bed for weeks, unable to speak. Claire would visit and bring food by the house. It took a while, but Misti finally arose from the depressive fog. As luck—or God—would have it, just in time for Misti and Richard to take in Josie.

Josie was thirteen at the time. Her parents chased work from California down through Arizona and into Texas. One night, they left her with no explanation. She was one more mouth to feed. Abandoned, she continued to live in the raggedy rent house in Kennedy Heights until the property owner reported the situation to Child Protective Services.

Claire remembered the late September weekend well. She was there the day Josie came through CPS, as she worked closely with social services in Houston. Maybe her heart was too soft, or made it was just the Lord's will, but Claire saw Josie as she came into the office with the workers and knew she was meant to help her. Claire had offered to let Josie stay at her place while the agency located a foster family.

The moment Claire saw Josie she knew she was special. It was hurricane season and the roads were packed. I-10 Westbound was a parking lot. Claire was prepared for the weekend warriors heading to Conroe after the work week, but not for the mass exodus of Louisiana residents evacuating because of the looming storm.

"There is no way we will make it home tonight," Claire thought. She was so close to Misti's exit that she did not even bother to call. She left the highway and headed to her best friends' place. Misti and Richard were already approved as foster parents, but they had not started fostering because of Misti's grief.

When time allowed, Claire loved to come to Misti's house. She loved the way the whole neighborhood looked like it was straight out of a magazine. As the inner-loop grew, the city pressured Houston Heights to gentrify, but residents resisted, concerned with historic preservation.

The Jacob's beautiful home was in the center of the Heights, an artistic community. Misti and Richard fit right in with their love of all things crafty. They even transformed their garage into a sky-lit pottery studio.

Misti had nothing nice to say to Claire for bringing a stranger, a child, unannounced into her home; however, by the next morning, Misti was out of her depressive state, and cooking breakfast for the first time in weeks. The smell of nutmeg cinnamon pancakes was all it took to surprise Claire and win Josie over.

In addition, when Richard arrived home that evening after a long day at the hospital to see Misti dressed and chicken spaghetti on the table, he deemed Josie was a keeper.

Misti thrived on having someone to take care of. Josie seemed like a gift from heaven, sent to bring order back into their broken lives. It was just supposed to be for one night, until the agency found another foster family, but Josie fit in so well, the agency approved her to stay. That was two years ago. Now, Josie was a member of the family.

Claire had no idea why Josie needed to see her so early in the morning, but it must have been important or Misti would not have called. Thankfully, it was Saturday and there was no school traffic. Claire effortlessly made the commute over to the Heights.

Sipping her Starbucks, Claire flipped on the radio. The news reporter gave a brief about a protest the night before.

More gun violence. More street mobs. Claire wondered if Cole had been there. After going back to Claire's the night before, he had taken a cab back to his apartment just in case the police department called him in as back-up to deal with the ever-increasing unrest in the city.

She did not want to think about it. She turned the radio off as she rounded the corner to Misti's driveway.

Josie was a shy, soft-spoken teenager. The pottery studio was her go-to place to regroup after she'd had a bad night. Josie sat at the wheel, nearly still, her tall frame hunched over in concentration as the wheel spun around. She had fleecy, curly black hair, common to her mother's African American side of the family, but she had the olive skin and dark hazel eyes of her Native American father.

The carport-turned-pottery-studio was a brilliant place with skylights that let in just enough light for the young girl to see her work. It was a therapeutic setting.

"Hey, Josie-Cat. What's up?" Claire asked as she let Maesters in behind her, his toenails clicking on the cold cement floor.

"Nothing." It was the only greeting from the almost still form at the wheel, a typical reply from a teenager.

Was this the reason I was dragged out of bed so early? Claire thought. Fighting frustration and impatience, she tried to connect with the girl again. "So, Misti said you wanted to talk to me. How are you?"

The spinning wheel never slowed. Josie refused to meet Claire's gaze.

"Everything okay?" Claire eased a little closer and leaned one hip on the wedging table, still sipping on her Starbucks.

Dust particles glittered as the sun filtered down through the skylight. It almost looked like dust from angels' wings. The soft light gently kissed all the vases and bowls in the studio, glinting off of Josie's curls.

"Morgan Ann's missing," Josie mumbled.

Those few words made a slight change in the atmosphere, and Claire became more alert and mindful of Josie. Feeling guilty for being so impatient, Claire reached out and touched Josie's thin forearm.

"This girl, Morgan Ann? She is a friend of yours?"

A slight nod.

"Best friend?"

"Not really."

"But you know her well enough to miss her, right?"

"Yeah."

Josie's mentors each added their own contributions and blessings to Josie's life, yet something was lacking. They had all let a vital ingredient slip through their fingers. Together, as they all tried to save Josie, they had mistakenly almost let her drown by not knowing her friends.

A train echoed from a faraway corner, yet close enough to hear. Everything seemed so cold and distant. Josie was keeping something back; Claire could sense it.

"How long has she been missing?"

"She ain't been at school in weeks."

"What about her parents? They haven't called the police?"

"I dunno. Prolly not. I hear they ain't never there. They are always working and they supposed to be fostering three other kids in elementary school."

Icy fingers of fear tickled Claire's heart. "Something about this doesn't make sense, Josie. The police should have been called for truancy. Surely, someone is out looking for her."

Frowning, Claire could not capture an image of Morgan Ann. Who was she? Claire mentally kicked herself for not knowing about Morgan Ann or her situation. She felt a drowning sensation. She had met so many of Josie's friends and teachers. Why couldn't she seem to place Morgan Ann?

Many people worked to care for Josie and make sure she did not fall through the cracks. It was all their responsibility to keep her safe. Knowing there was a young girl out there, a girl Josie knew, who was not cared for properly, made Claire feel sick.

With a deep breath, Claire promised herself she would be more vigilant. Losing people was a thing of Josie's past, and her feelings of abandonment were already overpowering enough. Richard and Misti tried to be the hedge that kept all the pain and fear at bay, but sometimes Claire was called in to help.

"What if something bad wrong happened to her, Claire?"

This was the first-time Josie had spoken her name since Claire arrived. Josie looked up as she opened her heart. Panicked hazel eyes met Claire's hypocritically strong and fearless brown ones.

"Josie-cat, we are going to do everything we can to figure out what's going on," Claire said as she gave the girl a comforting shoulder hug, staying clear of the wet clay.

Josie barely nodded. "She's talked about running away for a while now. I think she run away before. She got a boyfriend and everything."

"I'll talk to Cole tonight. We will check on her. Okay?" The vehement fervency in Claire's tone made Josie smile slightly, though her eyes were swimming with tears.

"Thanks, Claire." Josie's soft curls bounced as she nodded and a large grin crossed her face. Her smile showed the little space between her two front teeth, and Claire grinned back in response.

Maesters butted his large head against Josie's pant leg, as he snuffled and snorted.

"Let me wash up and I'll scratch your back," she said to the dog. Giggling, Josie went to wash her hands.

"Hey, keep an eye on him and make sure he does not eat any clay. I'm going to pop into the house and let Misti know I'm here." Claire went up the stairs to the back kitchen door. "I'll be right back," she called over her shoulder.

Even though she heard the sound of Josie's laughter behind her in the studio, Claire had no relief from the worry and sense of danger that had settled into her gut concerning Morgan Ann.

It was time to call Cole. She wanted to check on him from last night's protests anyway. Without hearing his voice, she would not be able to shake the spirit of fear that cloaked her.

CHAPTER 4

A cloud of powdered sugar and the smell of beignets welcomed Claire and her dog back to the apartment from their morning walk. Maesters pushed ahead with a bark, greeting Miss Daria Rainwater who opened the door.

"Hey, Miss Daria," Claire said as she greeted the thin, older woman with a hug.

"Hello there, Sha!"

Daria was from a little swamp-town south of New Orleans. Claire did not know the exact name of the place, but she imagined it was magical, with huge vats of gumbo, and mosquito nets everywhere. Daria's sharp, quick-witted tongue and silver hair pinned back in a coiled bun made Claire love her even more. Daria's dark-roasted laughter led Claire's imagination far away into the deep murky bayous.

Brilliant sunlight streamed into the apartment's bay windows, which overlooked the oak-lined street. The women happily chatted as they munched on beignets. Memories began to surface in the back of Claire's mind.

Long before Claire's mother passed away, Judge Sullivan hired Daria as his housekeeper, cook, secretary, Claire's nanny, and any other position she could possibly juggle. Daria was nothing like Claire's mother. She was a survivor. A planner. An organizer. A dream come true.

Judge Sullivan offered Daria a suite in his home, but she loved her quaint place in Fifth Ward French-town, the center of Houston's

Creole community. Regardless of her drive to work, Daria preferred to stay in her own home, close to others of Cajun culture.

After Claire's mother passed away, Daria would comfort Claire with scripture and prayer. That old Creole-French drawl slipped in as Daria prayed with Claire before bedtime. "If God sends us strong paths, He give us strong shoes as we go up the road. This present world is a fearful place, but if you are a child of the King, He been havin' you in His righteous hands."

Claire could still quote Daria's favorite verse, Isaiah 41:10, by heart. "Fear not, for I am with you; be not dismayed, for I am your God; I will strengthen you, I will help you, I will uphold you with my righteous right-hand."

Now that Claire was grown and had her own apartment downtown Houston, she would still occasionally come home to find duck salad and rice rolls waiting for her. It was take-out from Huynh's, her favorite Vietnamese restaurant. Daria would drop the food off for Claire, even though the motherly-woman grumbled about how Claire should eat more home-cooked meals, like her special shrimp gumbo or crawfish etouffee. Daria could not fathom going to bed thinking there might be a possibility that Claire was had gone without eating, which she often did due to her busy work schedule.

Today was one of the days Daria had let herself into Claire's apartment and had taken over her kitchen. The smell of the fried bread brought Claire back to the present moment. She shook her head from all the bombarding memories, and shooed Maesters out of the kitchen.

Daria had tuned the radio to a Christian station while she was cooking. The sing-song voice of a backwoods, East Texas preacher called out over the sound waves.

"Praise the Lord, saints. Keep your life free from the love of money, and be content with what you have, for He has said, 'I will never leave you nor forsake you.' Therefore, we can confidently say, 'The Lord is my helper; I will not fear; what can man do to me?' Hebrews chapter thirteen verses five and six confidently tells us . . ."

Claire firmly clicked the mute button on the radio remote, and the broadcaster's voice cut off mid-sentence. She smiled sarcastically at her wise-as-a-serpent friend. Not today. I cannot take any preaching today, Claire's eyes stated.

"This is the day the Lord has made, Sha. Let's rejoice and be glad in it!" Daria's perky voice rang out as she nodded toward the granite counter where another pile of beignets was waiting for a douse of powder sugar.

Hungry or not, Claire knew she had to help unless she wanted to start answering Daria's questions. They were questions she had no answers for, questions that kept swirling around inside her head.

"How you been sleeping lately?" Daria asked. "Are those dreams still comin' around?"

There they were, the questions Claire wanted to avoid. Daria met Claire's dark silence with a knowing glance and nod.

The older woman was aware of Claire's night terrors. Bedtime was the one thing Daria had gone out of her way to make special during Claire's childhood days, even though Judge Sullivan had told her not to coddle his daughter or give in to her fear. But the Creole lady knew a little something about fear. She knew what it was like trying to conquer the darkness. Lying in bed, sweating as streams of tears pooled onto the sheets was not the way to go about tackling fear.

To comfort little Claire, Daria would sit in a creaky rocking chair, cloaked in the darkness of night, rocking back and forth, making a comforting noise on the wooden bedroom planks. She would hum and whisper *"fais do do"* to the young girl, and the slippery shadows would have no choice but to retreat. The gloomy blackness would transform back into familiar objects at the sound of Daria's thick voice.

Just as David played his harp and sang psalms for King Saul, Daria would sing praises to the Lord until Claire was nestled in the arms of slumber. Daria realized long ago that God was more interested in the process than the product, that understanding transformed her walk with the Lord. Understanding God's priorities allowed her to concentrate on obedience to His Spirit. Caring for Claire and Judge Sullivan was just as much an act of love and service as it was obedience to the Lord. She knew she was in their lives for a reason.

"You know, Sha, we have prayer meeting t'night," Daria said as Claire began to sprinkle the powdered sugar on the New Orleans-style fritters. "That's all you need. A good talking with the Lord. He's all you really need, anyhow. He helped Daniel interpret dreams in the Bible."

Daria began humming an old hymn, wiped her fingers on a dishcloth and tucked it into her apron strings as she returned to her frying skillet.

Claire swallowed and searched for the right words to say. "I heard you, Ms. Daria. I have a meeting with Cole tonight. Dinner at six. We have to talk about a few things. I saw Josie today. By the way, I have some things to take care of for court Monday."

Daria gave Claire a sharp look as she shook her head at the younger woman. "The Lord won't put more on ya than ya can bear, Child. All that busyness is the devil's doing, overloadin' your plate like that. And that Cole Peretti needs to be at prayer meeting tonight almost more than you do."

Claire burst out laughing at that one. Just wait until Cole heard. "I'll make sure he knows that, Daria."

"The boy is runnin' from the will of the Lord. Maybe runnin' faster away than you are. God meant what he said, Claire Sullivan. Don't go trying to change or undo His words. You know you got the hand of the Lord on you and don't you go trying to fool me! Going through the motions of life won't ever satisfy. It's only when we bend down low, open our hearts, and say, "Jesus, it's You. Only You. There is no other. Sister Honeycutt taught that in Sunday school if you would'a been there last week."

The last bite of her beignets turned to sawdust in Claire's mouth. She'd heard it all before, and was not in the mood to deal with Daria shaming her into going back to church. That was the last place she wanted to be. How in the world was she to worship a God who allowed her father's murder to go unsolved? After all the detective work, and all the false leads, there was still no answer.

Daria hooted as she noticed the look on Claire's face. "Come see! Ya gonna be guests at the church Sunday, if the Lord be my help!"

Claire cleared her throat and placed the dish in the sink as delicately as she could. "Thank you for breakfast. It was delicious as always. Love you, Daria."

"I be praying for you, sha. You can get a fresh start! There is no expiration on the hope, plans and the dreams God has fer ya. God gives His hand to those that are down—gives a fresh start to those ready to quit. Dreams, prayers, and grace ain't got expiration dates. Today is the perfect day to believe."

Daria stood on her tiptoes to kiss Claire on the forehead before shooing her out of the kitchen. "I got all your laundry done. It is folded on the bed. You go on, now."

One thing Claire knew was that she would not be Daria's guest at the little downtown church, not if she could help it. Not this week, not next week, and not anytime soon.

Daria was wrong.

There was an expiration date on hopes, dreams, and God's plan. Claire understood Martha's attitude in the Bible story of Lazarus a little better now. Martha begged for Jesus to show up with a miracle, but He did not show up in time, and Lazarus died.

"If You had only been here, Jesus, then maybe my father wouldn't be dead," Claire angrily accused. The expiration date on Claire's dreams was the day her father died, leaving her alone. *"If you had only been here, things would be very different."*

CHAPTER 5

"The person who ignores slavery justifies it by
quickly deducting the victim is a willing participant
hampered by misfortune."

—D'Andre Lampkin

Pappadeaux's fried oysters and seafood platters were worth
waiting in line for thirty to forty-five minutes. As always, it was a
packed house, but it was still Cole and Claire's number one place to
eat. The couple enjoyed their time together and would talk during
the drive over and while waiting for a table.

Tonight was a special treat and the live band made the night even
better. Claire and Cole stood on the edge of the patio as they waited
to be seated. The humid air was thick with the promise of rain.

Claire thought Cole seemed distracted. It must have been a tough
case at work. Cole usually never said much about work, but Claire
could always tell when something was bothering him because the
creases in his forehead seemed to burrow deeper than usual.

As they followed the hostess to their table, Claire felt proud to
be on the arm of a man like Cole. He helped her settle into her chair
and sat down across from her at their table. She thought he looked
debonair in his open-necked white and red plaid shirt. The white in
the shirt complimented his dark skin.

"He is handsome to his core," she thought. *"I am so blessed. Blessed?
Ha! Daria is getting to me. When is the last time I thought I was blessed?"*

Shaking her head ruefully, she turned to Cole. "You'll never
guess what Daria wants us to do in the midst of our schedules!"

"What's that?" Cole asked tearing his eyes away from checking a text message on his phone. His sincere brown eyes were warm with curiosity.

"She wants us to go to church with her!" Not sure what his response would be, Claire held her breath as she watched Cole's face. Deep thoughtfulness reflected in his expression as he contemplated the idea. The look surprised her.

"Don't worry. I said, no," Claire said quickly with a laugh, grabbing a menu to hide her face. Why did she tell Cole what Daria had said? Surely, he would think the thought of going back to church was ludicrous.

"Does she still go to our church in Pasadena?" Cole asked nonchalantly as he picked up his menu.

Our church? Cole's comment puzzled Claire, but she was helpless to repress the memories that washed over her. She remembered lifting her hands in worship inside the of the gorgeous church as a massive choir sang a song that sent waves of goose bumps to her soul. She remembered how the people would worship and pray in the Spirit—how she would worship and pray, hands lifted as the massive choir sang with anointing. She thought of the music and the people dancing in the aisles, and the sound of voices speaking in various languages, praising God as the Spirit flowed through them.

"I—I'm not sure if she still goes there," she said. "Why do you ask? Actually, I think they started a little mission church downtown a couple of years back, and she started going there to help with Sunday school. You are not thinking of going back are you?" she said with a nervous giggle.

Claire's short, forced laughter met Cole's calm quietness, causing her some discomfort.

"Maybe. Why not, Claire?" He asked. The live band's loud saxophone and trumpets almost drown out Cole's quick response. He smirked and winked at Claire. "You are cute, you know that? Just think about it. What can it hurt to visit?"

Claire's mouth was still gaping open as a server walked up to take their order.

A half-hour later, Claire sighed as she wiped the last of the garlic sauce off her fingertips. Though Cole had thoroughly enjoyed his chicken and sausage gumbo, something was still weighing on his mind.

"Okay. Spill! What are you thinking so hard about over there?"

Cole smiled briefly. "I guess I'm having a hard time staying in the present." His sarcasm was as thick as the butter on the table. He reached a hand up to massage his forehead.

"Cole, I know you must be thinking about work, especially with the attacks on our police throughout the nation in the past several months."

Thoughtfully, he looked down. "Actually, it's a new case I've been studying for months now—dealing with victims of structural violence."

"Structural violence? You mean, like hate crimes? Like the violent and destructive street protests?" Claire searched her memory for anything related to the idea of "structural violence." Nothing seemed to stand out. He main focus was on immigration law and working to intervene for the many children and young people falling through society's cracks.

Cole sighed as if the weight of all Houston was on his shoulders. "Have I ever mentioned an Alfonso Suarez, or Lorenzo Morricone to you?"

"Just briefly. Why?"

"There have been stories told about those two. Crazy stuff."

"Stop it, Cole! You are acting like they are Keyser Sozes, or like this generation's Al Capone and Johnny Torrio. How crazy can it be? You make it sound like these are the villains in the scary stories gangsters tell their children to make them mind at bedtime."

"It's pretty crazy, Claire. The Harris County Police Department wants to perform raids on an area of the city where there is a lot of prostitution. The operation entails undercover officers entering the locations, posing as customers."

"Oh." Claire didn't want to seem worried, so she mustered up as much support as she could. "But that's great news, right?

Undercover work is not something you normally get to do. This is a great opportunity, and you get to put a stop to some of that stuff. What's wrong with that?"

Claire knew it was Cole's job to get the bad people off the streets. Though a part of her would always worry, she knew he was an excellent officer, and his team was one of Houston's finest. Stopping crime and cleaning up the city's prostitution rings was all that mattered. And if Cole could get a promotion for some undercover work, all the better. Going undercover would move him away from the street riots, and that was good.

"Here's the issue I have, Claire," Cole continued. "Suarez and Morricone are two of the top international human traffickers. They have an army of coyotes under them. Those two are worse than we even know. There are rumors circulating out there about the way these men toy with their prey. I've heard they even tattoo their initials onto the girls, like they are branding them as their property."

"What are you talking about? Tattoos, like a barcode or something? Hasn't the State Department been monitoring trafficking since '94?"

"Yeah, Claire. And you, little lawyer lady, of all people, should know that the United States is a transit, as well as a destination country, for trafficked persons. Almost twenty thousand females, mostly children, are trafficked into the country every year."

"Where are they coming from?"

"We figure that they are mostly coming from Honduras and Mexico. God only knows where else."

"Where are they going?"

"Florida. California. All over America."

Claire felt a dark stillness begin to choke her at the base of her neck as she listened to Cole. Faces of frantic young girls filled her mind, one mug shot after another, after another. Shaking her head to clear the images away, she tried to focus on the fact that she was with Cole, safe, in a restaurant. She blocked out all the background noise as she focused on his hushed whispers.

Cole shook his head and threw his napkin on the table, frustrated. "I don't like the idea of raids," he said. "If we raid these cantinas and bars looking for trafficked victims, then the women will retreat to less accessible places where it is difficult to bring in HIV prevention education. Without access to intervention services, these women may face a higher risk of HIV infection, and be more likely to spread HIV if they do become infected."

Claire felt her heart begin to race as she listened. She took a sip of her sweet tea.

"What does that have to do with you?" She asked. "They are going to be exposed no matter what. Isn't it more important to shut down their operation than to educate them about HIV? Especially if they are victims. Wouldn't the main focus be rescuing them? Human trafficking usually occurs around an international travel hub, but here in Texas? I know we have a large immigration population, but trafficking?"

"Yes, we do have a trafficking problem, Claire. How many kids have you seen come through the system that are not even legal citizens? Studies say there is over 244,000 American youth at risk for trafficking annually. The sex trade with trafficking victims in Houston is astronomical."

Claire's curiosity peaked. "Is that because of our location? Proximity to border?"

"Yes, and things have really amped up since Ima Matul spoke at the Democratic National Convention. Remember that?" Cole asked with a nod of his head. His eyes were wide with zealous concern.

"Yes, I do remember," Claire said. "She was one who was rescued out of labor trafficking. It was a huge victory. She educated us all about the realities of a world most of us really know nothing about."

"Pretty much since then, our team has started to step off into this dark world," Cole said. "We are near the I-10 Interstate, and the port of Houston is a popular point of entry for international criminals."

"There is an extremely low conviction rate for trafficking, even if you do find some of the victims you're looking for, Cole." Claire reminded him. "As harsh as it sounds, many people in the court system talk about trafficking victims as if they are all criminals."

"I know, but the two men I told you about are pure scum. I get it that we have to try to find them and stop them. They have coyotes that promise honest jobs to internationals, and as soon as the girls arrive, they strip them of their identification and take them to a breaking house. It's almost the same story Ima told."

Claire shook her head in disgust. She did not even want to ask about the breaking house, not tonight. It was so difficult for Cole to open the door to his mind and let her in to understand what he dealt with. Nothing was just black and white anymore. He was in the gray area. He could see the big picture, but the little parts often got in the way.

"We have to find these guys and stop them, somehow. But I don't want the trafficking victims to become victims of the system. If we find them prostituting, we have to arrest them." Cole took a deep breath as he reached for his glass of tea.

"Let's talk about laws for a minute," he continued. "Some laws not only criminalize sex work, but also deny victims essential human rights. As harsh as it sounds, some people think prostitutes do what they do because they make more money on their backs than they do working on their feet. I'm sure that's true for some of them, but many of them are victims—slaves—trapped with no way out.

"I have read many articles that estimate almost forty thousand teenagers run away every year. They account for many of the prostitutes we have on the streets. I'm not justifying what they do, but they're just trying to survive without an education. They fall victim to the street lords. Those guys use these kids' vulnerability to their advantage."

Claire's eyes lit up. "Cole, that reminds me! Josie told me about a school friend of hers that ran away recently. She wanted you to see if you could check out the girl's parents and see what's going on with that missing person's case. I can't believe I forgot to mention it!"

"More sweet tea, ma'am?" The server interrupted Claire.

Claire smiled and looked up. "Yes, please," she said as she held her glass out to the woman. Behind the server, a flat screen TV above the bar flashed a news headline announcing the abduction of a missing girl.

The photograph of the smiling girl on the TV caught Claire's attention. Her whole world began spiraling into darkness. She could feel the glass she was holding out for the server begin to slip out of her fingers. She heard Cole call out to her as she began to faint, falling out of her chair.

"*Oh, my God. That's her!*" Claire's thoughts were screaming, but she could not get the words out. The girl was plain, with mousy brown hair and brown eyes. Caucasian, almost nondescript, but Claire recognized her. It was the girl who silently screamed in her dreams on so many occasions. The girl on the TV was the same girl from her reoccurring nightmares.

Chapter 6

"Satan's greatest psychological weapon is a gut level
feeling of inferiority, inadequacy, and low self-worth.
This feeling shackles many Christians, in spite of wonderful
spiritual experiences and knowledge of God's Word.
Although they understand their position as sons and daughters
of God, they are tied up in knots, bound by a terrible feeling
inferiority, and chained to a deep sense of worthlessness."

—David A. Seamands, *Healing For Damaged Emotions*

A rush of humid, murky air snaked inside as Daria slipped in the front door of Claire's apartment.

"How's she?" Daria's hushed whisper echoed through the foyer hallway.

Cole closed the door leading to Claire's bedroom, shaking his head. "She cut her hand on the glass when she fell. I think she is finally asleep. Richard called her in a prescription a couple of hours ago. She was making herself sick from all the crying."

Daria moved down the hallway, placed her knitting bag on the overstuffed couch in the living room, and closed the drapes covering the floor to ceiling, wall-to-wall windows. Those windows were essential anywhere Claire lived. She had to have open space and wide windows, with no dark corners or shadows. She always let in the light.

"Well, you go get'cha some rest now. I'll stay on with her the rest of the night. She'll be fine."

Cole slumped into one of the generous leather chairs near the fireplace. An odd thought struck him. He had not made time to build a fire yet this year. Maybe Claire would like one. Placing his head in his hands, he groaned.

"Daria, what are we going to do? Claire is not getting better. We worked her father's case until it went cold. We have no leads. She can't accept the fact that Patrick's gone, and now, now she swears she's seeing visions of missing girls in her dreams."

Daria's lips tightened. "And ya don't believe her because . . . ?"

"You cannot be serious, Daria!"

"Why wouldn't I be serious? This is a serious matter, young man. Oh, Lord, have mercy! Give me the words and the patience to deal with this man. Let the words of my mouth, and the meditation of my heart, be acceptable in Ya sight, O LORD, my strength, and my redeemer."

Disbelieving, Cole stared in amazement at the aged woman before him. He did not know if he should laugh at her or take her seriously.

"She's exhausted, that is all. She works excessively. She sees tons of kids a year, deals with case workers, foster kids, foster parents, government employees . . ."

"Cole Peretti! Are you telling me that you don't believe in visions no longer?"

"Daria, that's not the point. I deal with things tangible. All I am saying is that she's over exerting herself. That's all this is. Fatigue."

Daria grabbed a footstool, placed it right in front of Cole, and sat down to look him straight in the face. Her wild, hazel green eyes glowed with an other worldly fire.

"Boy, let me remind you something," she said touching his chin with her wrinkled hands.

"You grew up in the faith. Your Grandma Lois didn't teach you the ways of the truth for nothin'. Just because that father of yours wanted you to follow in his footsteps, did not mean you had to abandon the call of the Lord. You had an anointing on your life, son. You were meant to preach the gospel, bind up the broken-hearted. Claire with you."

Cole shook his head and pushed back in his chair, but Daria had him cornered. No way was he getting away from this feisty, old lady.

"Daria. C'mon. Those were pipe dreams of a young boy infatuated with an idea. Attending seminary would have never paid my bills."

"You used to prophesy!"

"That's enough." Cole's voice grew hard. Those dreams died. He did not even feel worthy enough to rake through the ashes of his dead anointing. He sold those spiritual gifts long ago, like Esau selling his birthright for lentil soup.

"This isn't about me," Cole said. "This isn't about any of that. It's too late for all of that now. I'm too old. Those dreams died a long time ago. This is about Claire. She can't be this weak. She is just tired, that's all. Maybe we just need to take a few weeks off and go to Galveston, or go parasailing in Destin. Maybe rent a beach house, or even fly out to see my parents in Estes Park, Colorado. Dad retired a couple years back and I haven't been to see him at their new house yet."

Daria rolled her eyes, and pushed the footstool away from the chair with a snort. "This is just the beginning. I tell you, Cole Peretti! Jeremiah 33:3 says, 'Call on me and I will answer you and show you great and mighty things you do not know.' The hand of God is reaching out for the both of ya."

Cole watched as the tiny woman started down the hallway to Claire's bedroom where Maesters lay guard outside the door. He could see a tired weight on her frail shoulders.

"Cole, I'm telling you," she warned over her bony shoulder, "this is spiritual warfare. Spiritual warfare is very real. There is a fierce battle raging in the realm of the spirit between the forces of God and the forces of evil. Warfare happens every day, all the time. Whether you believe it or not, you are on a battlefield. You are in warfare. She's having dreams and visions for a reason. And, boy, you best get right. I don't want to see you become a casualty!"

CHAPTER 7

"Temptation is not his [Satan's] strongest weapon. Despair is. The enemy wants to make you believe that you are powerless over the circumstance of life, that God or no one else loves you and that you are all alone, you are going to lose your mind or that you are not smart enough to get out of this one. I believe this one of the enemy's most successful strategies. Simply because, if he can make you feel and believe that you are unloved, not needed, and alone; you become hopeless! But the enemy is a liar! And the Bible calls him the father of all lies."

—Michelle Word Hollis

She had the same dream again, but now something was different about it. This time, the girl tried to get up off the thin mattress. Angry, red blisters were broken open on each wrist, and blood oozed down her pale arms. Her tears made her hair stick to her bruised cheeks, making her gruesomely swollen, beaten face even more frightening. Nevertheless, her appearance did not stop the door from opening. Light spilled into the room as the girl's tormented eyes birthed fear once again.

Hoping the nightmares of last night were not real, Claire stayed very still, letting the memories of the night wash over her. The dream was so real she could feel the terror of bondage. She wished she could just hide under the blankets and let the entire world pass her by. The memory of seeing the girl on the restaurant's TV gave her a splitting headache. Relentlessly, the morning sunshine pulled Claire from her slumber.

"I know you're awake. Get up, child, and let's talk." Daria's voice was gentle and calming as it mixed with the sound of the rocking chair creaking on the wooden floorboards.

Groaning, Claire sat up in bed. Her disheveled black hair was stuck to the sides of her face with sweat, the way the girl's hair in the dream stuck to her face.

"Hey," Claire said. "Did you stay here all night?"

"Someone had to watch over ya. So the Lord and I decided we were up for the job." Daria's Bible lay open on her lap.

"I've been praying that the good Lord dispatch an army of angels to put up a hedge of protection 'round about this place all night."

Frowning, Claire stretched and got out of bed. She brushed a sweet kiss across Daria's forehead as she headed toward her bathroom. How could she ever make it without this lady?

"Thank you, Daria. It's Sunday. Don't you have church?"

"Yes. Glad you woke up. I need to head that direction. Did ya dream last night?" Daria asked before Claire could shut the bathroom door and ignore her.

"Yes."

"And you believe them dreams? You believe them dreams are real?"

"I don't know, Daria. It is so bizarre." The clammy fear clawed at Claire's belly once again. Tremors shook through her arms.

"You said you saw that missing girl on the news in your dreams, as you have many times in the past. That has to mean something. The Lord must be telling you something, sha. The closer to God's heart that you will allow yourself to get, the more you'll feel love for the unloveables in this world. I promise you, if you just keep going down this path towards the Lord, He will make everything clear. Every confusion come to light. Circle your problems with prayer."

Claire was silent as she listened to Daria and stared at herself in the mirror. Her normal olive complexion was pale. Dark swollen rings, the remnant of yesterdays panic attacks and crying, bagged under her blood shot brown eyes.

"Daria, I'm scared. I do not know what to do. I do not know how to address what's going on. I've seen that girl in my dreams. Horrible dreams. I swear I never met her before in my life but I know her. She is real, and now there are others, more girls, new faces."

"So, take it to the Lord, child. He said He would wipe away ya tears, and terrorize ya fears. Satan has no power over us except what we allow. Moment by moment, decision by decision you have these dreams for a reason. Circle 'em with prayer. Maybe it is time you figure out why you havin' 'em and get on with-it."

That's it? Just pray about it?" Claire shook her head. She had heard all that before. When was Daria going to let it go? Prayer was not enough. She had to do something. How in the world was she supposed to find this girl? Where would she begin looking?

"Daria . . ." Claire smiled as she saw the older woman begin to make her bed.

"Claire, if this girl is real, if any of the other girls' faces are real, then you have a job to do. I have met so many hurting people out there. So many people who are just masses, with no names. No one stops to hear their story. No one reaches a hand out to help. Maybe it is time you begin to reach out. We have prayer meeting Tuesday night. You should think about coming, and bring Cole with you. The good Lord knows he needs it."

Shutting the bathroom door, Claire decided a shower would clear her head. She did not want to hear Daria go on and on. She would talk to Cole about her dreams later. Surely, he could give her some advice, and together they could make everything work out for the good. At least that way she would be keeping her promise to Josie.

She was not sure about everything Daria said, but the one thing she knew was that she remembered what prayer was like. Prayer was the place where burdens shifted from her shoulders to the Lord's. If He could carry the weight of the world, then maybe He could carry her. Just this once more.

Chapter 8

"I cannot fail these girls by diverting my eyes from the invisible residue of slavery that clings to them like a shadow."

—Marquita Burke-DeJesus, *Radically Ordinary*

Monday morning came and went in a blur. It was a busy day talking to lawmakers, advising the organization, and completing a lot of paperwork, filing, and faxing.

Claire spent lunch with Misti Jacobs at Liquid Life. Richard finally agreed it was time to send Josie back to school. The girl seemed to be in better spirits, but Misti was still worried. Claire promised to let her know what she found out from Cole later that day.

Before she knew it, Claire's day was over. She was on her way to her car when she got the phone call from Cole.

"I have some info for you. I did not realize it, but the police have been looking for this Morgan Ann Bishop for a while now. She is a foster kid. We have already talked with the foster parents. She tried to run away before. It's a typical story . . ."

"Hello to you too," Claire softly laughed. What a strenuous day it had been, but she was interested in what he was saying. "Tell me everything you know."

"Hi, sweetheart," Cole said, pausing briefly. Claire could hear the smile in his voice. "Well, Morgan Ann is a product of our screwed-up society," he continued in his train of thought. "Her bio-mother was a 13-year-old rape victim. The mother dumped her newborn in the dumpster behind a Spanish church in Baytown. CPS was notified when the preacher's wife found the baby. They placed her in foster care, and she moved around a bit. She was at her last home since she was ten years old. She's fourteen now.

"She fights bulimia and cuts herself. She has been in counseling for over a year. Things started to look up when the foster parents told us that Morgan Ann recently was involved with a boyfriend. I asked the chief to let us in on the case, so Joels and I are headed over to talk with the boyfriend, if you want to tag along."

Ken Joels had been Cole Peretti's partner for years. The tall African American man was intimidating to look at. Other officers said he reminded them all of a brick wall that could run. Claire worried a lot less about Cole when Joels was with him. The man had worked many years with her father, Judge Patrick Sullivan. To Claire, seeing Joels was almost like seeing a remnant of her father still left behind on earth. She loved him dearly, and thought of him as an old soul.

"Sorry, I just rushed into all of those details, Claire. I knew you would want to know. We have had men on the streets all week with her picture. We're going to find her. We are covering all the bases. Her boyfriend, Jackson Miller, is supposed to be the last one Morgan Ann was with. They have been dating for a few months now, according to some of the kids at school. The foster parents never met him. He is a dropout. Quit school last year. Possible a minor drug dealer. Josie has heard of him."

Claire could hear Cole's car revving up on the other side of the phone, and the deep baritone voice of Joels in the background.

"Yes," Claire confirmed. "Josie mentioned a boyfriend to me. Come get me. I'm headed back to my apartment now. I want to go with y'all to meet this guy."

"We're on our way now to get you, Love. See you in a few. We will be going toward Sharpstown."

"Sharpstown! Seriously? Isn't Sharpstown the community with over five hundred burglaries last year?"

"Yes, and almost three hundred stolen cars in the matter of one year. There are other reasons we may be interested in this kid, Jackson Miller. He already has a rap sheet. Burglary, drug bust. He has to know where Morgan Ann is. We'll start there."

Twenty minutes later Claire hopped into the backseat of Cole's car and they started on their way. The three professionals did not talk much on the drive over. Claire stared at the photograph on her lap, memorizing each trace of the young Morgan Ann's face, from the brown strands of hair, to her brown eyes, to her pale skin and slight dimples. She had a small scar on the edge of her chin, and a freckle above her left eyebrow. Every detail embedded itself into Claire's brain.

"*I will find you,*" Claire promised the girl in the picture silently. "*With the Lords' help, I will find you! I promise you. No matter how long it takes.*"

Sharpstown was a radically mixed neighborhood with a strong Vietnamese community. The area had more total crimes than any other section of Houston. It was a colorless, sprawling neighborhood centered on the Southwest Freeway and Bellaire Boulevard. At least nine thousand people were packed into each square mile, most living in a disarray of large apartment complexes. There were three times more people per mile than any other Houston neighborhood.

Claire looked out over the gloomy landscape searching each sad, long face as they drove by. Could one be Morgan Ann?

Joels pulled into a gravel parking lot at the rear of a dilapidated brick two-story. "Jackson Miller is supposed to live in 248-B. It is on the second floor. The apartment is rented out to a Wayne Touts," he said as he carefully opened the car door and slipped out.

The building looked condemned. Joels headed toward the back fire escape, which lead up to the second floor landing.

"Stay here," Cole called over his shoulder to Claire as he followed Joels. "I'll send you a text letting you know when it will be okay to join us." He began to climb the rickety, rust-iron steps. When they reached the second floor, Joels grabbed the exterior door leading into the hallway. The door barely clung to its hinges and looked as if Joels could rip it off the wall with the slightest touch.

Claire sat locked in the backseat of the car, surveying the miserable neighborhood's landscape. Where once there had been such hope, now there was a resounding aura of despair and dejection. Time had overtaken everything. Weeds began to conquer and eat away at broken sidewalks. Refuse and litter replaced yard decor. Street signs were riddled with bullet holes, and the lone gas station's graffiti screamed that despite everything, "ALL LIVES MATTER!"

Claire remembered a line from an old book that said, "This was the ghetto: where children grow down instead of up." If there ever was a place to hide, this was definitely the gloomiest jackpot. What was Morgan Ann running from? Had she ran away as Josie assumed, with her boyfriend, or was she taken? Was she even alive? Surely, she had to be alive, after all the dreams. Claire surely would have felt otherwise in her spirit.

Claire watched a brief drug pass between the window of a rusty Oldsmobile to someone riding on a bike, just as she received the text from Cole. She got out of the car and quickly went up the dilapidated metal stairs leading to the second floor.

Easing around the broken door, a myriad of smells immediately assaulted her. Sharpstown had become a melting pot for poor immigrants, so the smell was no surprise to her. It smelled like greasy fried pork, mixed with the sweet odor of marijuana, mixed with cloying incense, mingled with an odd aroma of Vietnamese noodles. All of which interlaced with the dying smell of mildew.

Cautiously edging down the filthy corridor littered with rat droppings, newspapers and used condoms, Claire could hear a blaring Spanish television station and the weak cry of an infant. She finally continued far enough down the hallway to recognize Cole's tenor voice. Knowing he was present brought immediate relief and a sense of security. She felt safe.

With a light tap on the ajar door, Claire eased inside the tiny apartment. It was like any obligatory apartment. A slight foyer opened into a living area. There was a kitchenette on the side, and two doors to the rear of the room, which was obviously a bathroom and bedroom. There was a smoker's balcony overlooking the street below. The glass sliding door stood open, allowing the afternoon air to stir into the stale apartment.

Claire expected the apartment to be in worse condition than it was, but it was not clean by any means. The beige walls were littered with old nail holes from tenants long since gone. The kitchenette was empty other than mildew creeping up the sink and backsplash. The overflowing trashcan, vomited empty cigarette packs and beer bottles onto the floor.

Joels and Cole, like two avenging angels, flanked a ratty-holed couch that sagged from a broken spring.

Jackson Miller sat on the couch. He was a lanky, thin, sullen African American boy. Anger and resentment dulled his eyes. Claire stared at the unimpressive young man. She guessed he must have been about nineteen years old.

"What would a young girl like Morgan Ann find so attractive about this boy?" Claire thought. Jackson's long dreadlocks lay matted against filthy, acne-pocked skin. The boy fidgeted with a tongue ring as he sat staring at the warped linoleum floor, his skinny arms folded over his chest.

Joels clapped a bear-sized hand onto the boy's shoulder, startling him into a jump. Cole smiled and winked at Claire as Joels spoke.

"Miller here says he's never met a Morgan Ann Bishop before. Even though we know they were in high school classes together before this loser dropped out."

Chuckling, Cole squatted down beside the couch and stared into the boy's hazy eyes. "So, Son, we think you may want to start talking."

"I ain't got nothing to say to no poe-lice," he mumbled staring down at his sneakers.

"Nice Vans," Claire said to herself, curious where he got money for shoes like that.

"Whose place is this?" Joels demanded.

"Buddy of mine, Wayne's place."

"And you say Morgan Ann Bishop's never been here before?" Cole asked as he stood to peer out the balcony to the street below. He could see a few guys talking to a couple of hookers on the corner. They barely looked of the legal age.

"I told ya, man. I ain't never seen her before. Don't know any Morgan Ann Bishop." The boy shrugged off Joels' hand and tried to stand up.

"Not so fast, squirt. Explain to us how all her friends knew you were her boyfriend?" Joels asked pushing the kid back onto the couch.

Jackson tried not to show the nervous fear he began to feel as he mumbled explicit curses.

"And we tracked her cell phone to this apartment building," Cole added turning back to the couch from looking at the street. His body cast a long shadow across the room.

"Here's the deal, punk. We have brought you a lawyer. Meet Ms. Claire Sullivan. We suspect you've murdered Morgan Ann Bishop, left her for dead somewhere, hid the body. You might wanna get to know Ms. Sullivan a little better because we are about to arrest you and you are going to need a lawyer." Cole said with a confident smirk nodding for Joels to get his handcuffs.

Jackson's weak chin began to tremble as his eyes raced from one serious face to another. His mouth gaping open he tried to speak.

"W-what? I didn't do that. She fine. She okay. She just went out. Went to work. Yeah, she went to work. She be back tonight. She told me to take her with me. She wanted to get a job. Get away. That's all. Honest."

"Words mean nothing until they are proven and shown," Joels snarled, yanking the boy up by his ripped collar.

"Okay. Okay. Chill, dude. So, I helped her run away. Big deal. She said she knew some people down here who would let her dance or somethin'. She met someone online who offered her a job off the Backpage website. Even though she ain't legal age or whatever, she could do the job. She just turn fifteen and didn't wanna live with her foster folks no more." The words stumbled out of Jackson's mouth, jumbling together almost faster than he could get them out.

"And you never thought it was a trick?" Claire caught herself saying. Her heart speeding up. Could they be this close to finding Morgan Ann? How did her dreams play into all this?

"I'm just givin' her a place to stay. That's all. We stay here with Wayne. This Wayne's place."

Cole turned to look at Claire, his lips tight with annoyance. Jackson tried to get away from Joels' grasp and began to yell.

"Brutality. Help! Po-lice brutality!"

"You're a pathetic joke, boy." Joels growled in disgust balling up his ham-sized fists.

"Dude, I ain't done nothin' wrong. She be back later, I swear."

"Where does she work?" Claire demanded.

"It's some strip club off Grand Avenue—Adolf's Lair."

Joels shook his head and dropped Jackson on the floor in a heap. "Stay here, scumbag. We definitely have more to talk to you about later." Joels growled, striding out the apartment door.

Cole turned to Claire with a serious look as they headed out the door and down the hallway to the car.

"In so many of Houston's sex slave cases that we have encountered this far, the only lure a trafficker needs to convince a girl to join them is simply offer them a job. That is all the pimps need, just for the girls to walk into their web of deceit. Work is the enticing candy these people use to tempt them into captivity. They think they'll make money and be independent. They are completely deceived. Morgan Ann must have let her guard down. I am going to make a call and get an officer to keep watch over this place so this kid, Jackson, doesn't try to run."

CHAPTER 9

"Love is patient, love is kind. It does not envy, it does not boast,
it is not proud. It does not dishonor others, it is not self-seeking,
it is not easily angered, it keeps no record of wrongs.
Love does not delight in evil but rejoices with the truth.
It always protects, always trusts, always hopes, always
perseveres. Love never fails. But where there are prophecies,
they will cease; where there are tongues, they will be stilled;
where there is knowledge, it will pass away."

—1 Corinthians 13:4-8

Cole closed the Bible his mother bought him for Christmas and laid it down on the passenger seat of his police car. He stared out at Houston's smoggy night skyline. The day had passed quickly, and he was waiting for Joels and the rest of the department to finish up the details concerning the raid on Adolf's Lair. It would be a big bust, and he hoped they would find Morgan Ann Bishop and get her home.

While he sat in his car waiting, he felt the tug and appeal of the Spirit of the Lord to return to his calling, return to his church, and renew his life in Christ. He felt the drawing of God's Spirit quite often. Much had changed since he was a teenager. Over the years, his heart had somehow sadly hardened.

Cole's desire to preach was trumped by his militant father's desire for him to "make something of himself." He placed Bible College on hold. He placed God on hold. At the time, he thought if the police academy did not work out, he could always chase the dreams and plans God had for him later.

As life and the winds of time would have it, Cole was excellent at whatever his hand found to do. His boyhood dreams of preaching revivals across America faded into distant melancholy aches that he hid behind his Houston police uniform. He tried hard not to think about his longings as he patrolled protests and street rallies full of angry citizens who seemed to be on a warpath. Those were the moments he prayed the hardest. He did not want to die on the streets. He just wanted to make it home after each shift.

Running his long slender fingers through his disheveled jet black hair, Cole breathed out a sigh. He never expected his God-given promises to lay dormant in his heart and die. He remembered carrying a promise from God that he would preach. He prayed for people to be delivered from demonic powers and addictions.

He wanted to hear the voice of the Lord again. He wanted to release all his pent up anger. He did not want to be the person he had become anymore. He just was not sure if Claire was ready or not to start attending church again. He smiled at the thought of Daria warning them about not getting married yet.

"While you busy making plans, life happens!" She would say.

A hollow feeling settled in his heart. He did not want to fail Claire. He had to have her in his life. She completed him. Sure, they planned to get married one day, but the timing was never right. Life was convenient that way.

Cole knew without any doubt that he had a call to preach on his life and he was not sure if that would fit into Claire's plans. In the stillness of his heart, doubt began to speak to him. What if he and Claire did not make it as a couple? What if she did not want to go back to church? What if she refused to give her life back to the will of God with him?

Circumstances seemed to always arise. They led such busy lives and schedules. He needed to spend time in the presence of the King of Kings. His identity was once found in the Savior but no longer. He needed to find himself again.

The book of James had always been his favorite New Testament book to read. His favorite line included the definition of what pure religion was all about. Pure religion consisted of visiting the fatherless and the widows, Cole had that part down, or so he thought.

He was a police officer. He was supposed to be compassionate, right? But it was the last part of that verse that was eating away at his thoughts . . . "Remain unspotted from the world."

Was Cole unspotted? Or had he allowed the world to completely captivate him?

Cole gazed out into the night, hoping that God knew his prayers even when he could not find the words to say. Cole was not sure what tomorrow would hold, but he could feel apprehension in the air. Was he afraid to die? As a police officer, that was a question he was met with often especially now with the brutal attacks happening all over the country against the police force.

Cole clinched his fist together as he remembered an old quote he had heard by Christopher Hitchens. "It will happen to all of you at some point. You'll be tapped on the shoulder and told, not just that the party is over, but slightly worse: the party's going on, but you have to leave."

All Cole knew was that if he did not get right with the Lord in a short space of time, he might not have much longer to make the choice.

Setting his face like a flint, Cole finally took a deep breath and picked up his phone. He rapidly sent a text message to Claire before he could reason himself out of it.

"Claire. We are going to church with Daria next Tuesday. Don't argue about it. Just do it. Love you. I will have a big surprise for you soon."

CHAPTER 10

"The backslider likes the preaching that wouldn't hit the side of a house, while the real disciple is delighted when the truth brings him to his knees."

—Billy Sunday

The following evening, Cole was finishing up the last of the frustrating paperwork from the Adolf's Lair raid. He was thoroughly disappointed with the little information that Joels supplied on the forms.

Yes, three johns arrested. There were six underage girls arrested for possession of marijuana, and a couple of older women arrested for prostitution, but nowhere had Joels mentioned the owner of the building, or if he found Morgan Ann in the process.

A team was interviewing the women now about Morgan Ann. Cole found it disturbing that the main reason they had raided the building was not addressed in the reports at all. His thoughts went back to the night he and Claire were having dinner at Pappadeaux's and how he tried to explain to her why he felt raids never worked.

Cole had worked to edge out human trafficking since Patrick Sullivan was alive. He was the one judge who let the coyotes have it. He put at least six men away for life for abducting and selling girls, human trafficking, and transporting kidnapped persons across the border. There were so many they had caught, yet there was so much left to do.

Sullivan believed in Cole, and together they were making a difference in Houston. Judge Sullivan always told him that God's work, done in God's way, never lacked supply. But today Cole Peretti was feeling a lack of help. A lack of support.

It felt as if he alone were facing the giant called human trafficking. He felt as if he were going to be squashed. It felt like he would never find Suarez and Morricone. Why did he even try? There was so much to do, and not enough man power.

There was not enough awareness to push back the darkness. More than ever, Cole felt compelled to be in the house of God. He could not wait to be back inside a church. Tonight was the night. *"Claire and Daria should already be there,"* he thought.

The church Daria attended was downtown Houston, nestled between a barbershop and a beauty supply store. The storefront church had a large sign on the window, which read: "Welcome to a Sanctuary of Hope and Strength."

The cold November wind had picked up tremendously by the time Cole arrived. He quickly parked his car, dusted off his pant legs, and rushed toward Claire's car, smiling. Cole opened the car door, and helped Claire out, taking her by the hand. With a quick kiss, Claire looked up into his warm eyes. He could tell she was just as nervous as he was.

"Think the walls will fall in on us? You know how bad of sinners we are," Claire joked, trying to lighten the mood. It was Claire's first time entering a church since her father's funeral. Her mind went back to that despised day.

The funeral had been in the spacious Pasadena church where Judge Sullivan was a deacon. The building held fifteen hundred people and was completely packed out. Ushers set out metal folding chairs to accommodate the mass of people.

Through a hazy fog, Claire remembered what the church was like at the funeral. She looked around and saw law officers, fellow judges who worked beside her father in court, and people who should have been in jail. Some of those people once committed minor offenses, but her father showed mercy to them and sent them to counseling classes, treatment centers, and to church to give them a second chance. They were all at the funeral.

Claire was amazed at how many people hugged her that day and praised her father. A lot of people stood to speak about how their lives were better because they were given one more chance to make things right—all because of Judge Patrick Sullivan's mercy.

Strains of music from an organ and a keyboard played as early church goers entered the small rented building to pray. The music awakened Claire from her memories as she watched people shake hands and welcome each other as they entered the building.

"Daria, go in ahead of us," Claire called out. "We'll be in a minute. I need to speak to Cole," she said as emotions rose in her chest.

She felt as if she were wading through mud. She had been angry with God for so long. How could she just enter His house and forgive Him for taking her father and allowing his murderers to live free? The thought of that was unacceptable.

Cole interrupted her thoughts. "C'mon. Let's go in. It cannot be that bad. We will listen to the preacher exhort for a moment. Then we will find a place to pray. Prayer eases the mind. Church can't be that bad," Cole promised as he rubbed Claire's arm and led her along the sidewalk up to the church building.

"Then we will leave," he said. "Maybe we will even have enough time left over to run by Huynh's for take-out," he joked. With a short burst of relieved laughter, Claire nodded as they stepped inside the glass door.

"Welcome, Claire Sullivan." A warm, dusky voice enveloped Claire like a mother's hug, and resounded through her spirit. A tall black woman with striking features called out Claire's name again.

Turning around, Claire was surprised and happy to see Shana Keni. The gorgeous woman was a friend Claire had met many years ago.

Shana Keni was an immigrant who had moved to America from Sierra Leone in 2002. The civil war there left more than fifty thousand people dead, much of the country's infrastructure destroyed, and over two million people displaced as refugees in neighboring countries. Shana counted it as a blessing to become an American citizen.

"Well, look at you! You haven't changed a bit," Claire said with a smile. How she had missed this woman. "You remember Cole, don't you?"

"Well, of course! I have been praying for both of you! You are an answer to many prayers just by being here tonight. Let the Lord touch you."

"Thank you, Sister Shana. I am grateful to be here."

"Come in when you are ready." The lanky woman turned to walk into the sanctuary. Pausing, she swiveled around on her foot with an intent stare. "Claire, I have a word from the Lord for you. I know this may be a little intense because you have not been in church in a long while, but I feel impressed to tell you something the Lord put on my heart for you."

The hair on Claire's arms stood up. She did not dare breathe as she waited for Shana to speak. Cole stood by silently.

"The Lord wants me to remind you of the time that He was able to do that first miracle in Cana, only because he was invited to the wedding. You must invite the Lord into your life, and then He will bring the miracle. When you look for God, He will find you. Look for Him, He is searching for you."

"Thank you, Sister Shana," Claire murmured as she fought to keep her emotions in check.

Shana's ebony eyes seemed to glow with a holy fire. She squeezed Claire's arm, and with a firm nod toward Cole, she turned and slipped into the church sanctuary. Cole and Claire following.

It was a small Tuesday night crowd. Maybe thirty-five or forty people were there. Claire could see Misti and Richard even though the lights were dimmed to encourage people to pray instead of talk. Josie grinned and waved Claire over to sit with them.

The service began with worship. A praise team sang. There was a moment for people to call out their prayer requests. Claire placed a twenty in the offering plate as it was passed down the aisle. A brief moment was given for two or three people to testify and give a praise report for answered prayers, then the pastor stood to preach.

The Hispanic pastor, Reverend Manguia, welcomed the crowd and began speaking. "There are three key individuals you must forgive if you want to make it to heaven with a clean and pure heart. First of all, you must forgive your oppressors, those who do evil against you. You must forgive them even if they never give you an apology.

"I heard a story once of a young man who came to realize he had a rat in his house. Therefore, to solve the problem of getting rid of the rat, he burned the house down in hopes of killing the rat. That is the same way it will be with you. You will burn your life down around your ears if you decide to 'get rid of your enemies' by hating them. You will destroy yourself.

"When we forgive someone, we're not endorsing what happened to us or what they did, we are not saying we agree with the choices they made or that what happened to us was acceptable. We're just saying that we're not willing to be bitter any longer.

"When we forgive our debtors, we are declaring that we will begin living life in freedom, instead of in emotional bondage. The Bible clearly says that we do not wrestle against flesh and blood, but against principalities, against powers, against the rulers of darkness of this age, against spiritual hosts of wickedness in the heavenly places."

Claire's thoughts turned inward. Forgive her father's killers? That was ludicrous. What had her father done so wrong that he had to be killed? Who hated him so much that they had to put a stop to his justice?

Looking even further down the corridors of her broken heart, Claire had a painful thought. Forgive her mother for being so weak? Forgive her for giving in to cancer and death without a fight? Forgive her father for being too strong?

Reverend Manguia stepped out from behind the podium and began to walk down the aisles among the people as he continued to talk to them.

"You must also forgive yourself. You must forgive yourself for any past mistakes and failures that you cannot forget."

"*Forgive myself?*" Claire thought. What audacity this man had for telling her to do such things. He didn't know her!

"Yes, forgive yourself. Forgive yourself for hating, for being angry at God, angry at the circumstances that left you all alone," the preacher said, stopping a few pews short from where Cole and Claire sat.

A chill went down Claire's spine. Surely, he could not be talking to her or about her situation. This was all just a coincidence.

"And finally, you must forgive God. God failed to live up to your expectations, and you must forgive Him for that.

"Start sticking up for the people Jesus stuck up for, even when it costs you friendships, family members, or even your own dreams. Will you decide tonight to follow in the dust of your Master's feet? Will you go where he leads?"

Did anyone hear the audible intake of breath as Claire gasped? Her face grew hot with embarrassment. Claire bit her lip and resented the tears she had to fight back as the soft melody from the keyboard soothed her thirsty soul.

The pastor continued to talk. "The God of the whole universe has a master plan. From the beginning of time, through the eons and ages, He knew one day you would need a Savior. So as the compassionate God that He ever is, with tender mercies renewed for us every morning, God robed himself in flesh and came to earth as the man Christ Jesus. He became the lamb slain so our sins, though they be many, would be washed away by the priceless blood shed on Calvary's cross. Tonight, we have another opportunity to gather around and worship the King of kings and the Lord of lords."

Claire had heard this all before, but it had been so long ago. She could begin to feel the sweet presence of the Lord. It felt like a gentle tug on her heart. She was not completely sure if she wanted to run out the glass double doors into the cold night, or run the few feet to the church's altar and pray. Such a struggle battled within her.

Fighting the urge to cry, Claire reached for Cole's reassuring hand as the praise singers began to softly sing.

Amazing grace how sweet the sound
That saved a wretch like me
I once was lost, but now I'm found
Was blind, but now I see

Cole tugged on Claire's hand, "Let's go."

"I don't want to leave," Claire's heart cried. For the first time in many years, her thirsty soul was drinking from God's well. She never realized just how dry and empty her heart had been. The sweet Comforter was tugging, drawing, wooing her back into His presence. She could almost feel the presence of angels as they ministered to individuals throughout the room.

"Let's go," Cole repeated urgently, as he led Claire out into the aisle down to the front of the church to pray. He had not meant to leave the service.

Part of Claire struggled, wanting to resist. She wanted to hide from the stares of the church members, but she knew what she had to do. She knew there was a God-shaped hole inside her heart. An ache deep within that only God could completely fill. Jesus Christ was the only one who could completely dispel the evil spirits that haunted her in her nightmares. He could become her Prince of Peace once again.

There were several altar workers, people who helped others pray, already worshiping and praising the Lord. Among the prayers workers were a set of elderly twins that Claire remembered from the Pasadena church, Tina and Nina Nobles. One was blind, the other was deaf, but that did not stop them from praying.

In fact, they were a mighty duo, praying with anyone who came to the altar. The women spent most of their days in the church, praying, fasting, and allowing the Lord to use them to prophesy. Claire could remember as a youth, watching the twins' link arms, shout, and dance in the aisles under the influence of the Holy Ghost.

Reaching the altar, Cole released Claire's hand and to her surprise, he began to weep as he raised both hands high above his head and prayed. Closing her eyes as she felt the delicate pressure of Daria's hands on the back of her shoulders. Claire began to pray.

"Lord, I am sorry. I am so sorry. Please forgive me for doubting You. Please forgive me for hating those men who did this to my family. Please forgive me. I want You back in my life. I want to know You again."

Claire raised her hands to cover her face and began to sob. She could feel movement around her and a soft hand that felt like old onion skin touched her arm. Several minutes went by before she heard the voice.

"Claire, I prophesy unto you. When God is with you, you are with the Healer of our bodies. The Helper, the Defender, and the Rescuer. When you are right with the Lord, You are with the One who turns every mess into a miracle of goodness. God's arms have you. Let go and let God take control." The voice of Nina Nobles surrounded Claire like a blanket.

She could hear Cole begin to speak in another language he had never learned before. She knew that speaking in tongues was the evidence of the Holy Ghost, and of submitting one's life completely to the Lord and allowing Him to live in the heart.

Claire wanted to be filled with the Spirit again. She wanted to Lord to write His name on her heart once again. She knew she was a daughter of the King. She knew she needed to come home.

Tina Nobles was holding Claire's arm on the other side of her. "God's love toward us is not determined by who we are or what we do, but by who He is. He loves you, Sister Claire. Let the Lord love you again."

Reverend Manguia stood quietly beside the couple. Claire could feel him lay his hands on her head and on Cole's head. He began to pray for them as a couple and asked the Lord to fill them with the Holy Ghost once again. Claire could hear the minister speaking in tongues. It was a beautiful angelic-like language.

"Sister Claire Sullivan, great grace will be upon you. Do not fear being overtaken by the past hurts, past failures, past sins. Your sins have been forgiven. Rise up now. This is an invitation to walk closer to Jesus Christ. There are places He desires you to go, but you cannot go if you stay at a distance from Him."

The sweet presence of the Lord swept over Claire, and she felt cleansed. She felt whole again. Uncontrollable tongues began to roll forth out of her mouth. With a strong voice, she began to speak in a language that she had never learned before.

Claire's eyes were tightly closed, but she could hear Cole rejoicing and leaping for joy beside her. Then she was caught up in the Spirit and nothing around her mattered. The Lord who had knocked on her heart's door for so long was here to remove all fear and doubt. She was finally swinging open wide that door of her heart and letting God in for good.

CHAPTER 11

"We live in a world that is watching the church with one eyebrow raised. When Hollywood is viewed as doing more to feed the hungry and fight human trafficking than the church, we need to take a hard look at what we're doing and ask if it's enough. Jesus taught that when others see our good deeds they would assign value to God (Matthew 5:16). I can't help but think that the same is true for his church."

—Brandon Hatmaker, *Barefoot Church: Serving the Least in a Consumer Culture* (Exponential Series)

The following day, Daria ask Claire to meet her for lunch. Claire planned to take an early lunch to meet Daria downtown. It was an unfamiliar address Daria had texted to her, but it was not too far from where Claire worked.

She had to call an Uber driver, her poor Fiat was being pushed further and further down the list of things that needed to be cared for.

As the Uber pulled up to the small, stucco building at the address Daria had given her, Claire's curiosity peaked. She had already paid for her ride and tipped the driver, with a simple tap on her phone app before stepping out of the car. She thanked the driver and turned around to the building. What was this place?

"Daria? Hello? I'm here."

The building was in disarray, a mix of renovation and reconstruction. The entrance was a small room, barely a five-by-five lobby. All the walls were completely torn down except for the beams, which were oddly enough glued over with small sheets of paper. Looking closely, Claire noticed someone had glued pages ripped from an old Bible onto the beams.

"Claire, come see!" Daria called out from down the long hallway. A beautiful Hispanic woman followed her. "This is Sister Rita Manguia, the pastor's sister," Daria explained. "She is gonna be our guide today."

"Guide? Where are we?" Claire asked, smiling at the two women.

"Praise the Lord, Sister Claire. I am so excited to see what the Lord is doing in your life," Sister Rita Manguia said.

"You were there last night?" Claire asked, not recognizing the woman.

"Yes, ma'am. My daughter, Azalea and I did not get to greet you, but she is here today as well. You will have to meet her. Come see what is going on."

Sister Rita Manguia escorted the women into a dimly lit room in a state of remodeling. "I will tell you all about it as we walk. First of all, you must know that I am a part of a church group called J.O.Y which stands for Just Older Youth."

"Oh, I like that! The young at heart," Claire joked.

"Yes. Yes. We are a group of older women and men who are involved in missions' endeavors around Houston. We help the homeless, or whoever needs our help. We go to parks and feed the hungry latchkey kids. We bring coffee to the homeless missions early in the mornings. We visited the widows, and just make so many new friends.

"We visit the battered women's shelter, and the children's home. Since becoming more aware of human trafficking in our area, we have ventured out and began to help the prostitutes more as well, making hygiene bags for them, and passing out information and help line numbers."

Rita smiled; her dark brown eyes bright with fervency and her voice full of hope as she continued sharing her burden. "Human trafficking is the fastest growing criminal industry in the world. The FBI cites I-10 as the highest rated corridor for human trafficking. We have spent a lot of time praying in this little building. Our goal here is to pray for the trafficking victims: strength, freedom, safety, hope, help, healing, and restoration. We pray for their families and that they can be reunited."

Daria grabbed Claire's hand and stopped her in the middle of the hallway. "Through our restoration work, we have had the incredible privilege of seeing this happen over the months of caring for these women. If Jesus were to love any of us, any one at all, I think He would love the trafficked ones the most. He knows their pain of betrayal, and His body was sold as well. Judas betrayed Him for money. That amount money he was given was only enough to buy a slave back then. These girls are sold too, slaves."

"Wow, Daria. That's so true. I never thought of it like that."

Shaking her head to clear her emotions, Rita smiled at Claire. "You know, Jesus never spoke as plainly to anyone as he did to the little woman at the well in John chapter four. He told her he was the Messiah who had come to save the world. When you begin to look for God, He will find you."

Claire froze. Those words resonated with her heart. He will find you. She could see faith all over Rita's face.

"You know, my new friend, Claire," Rita continued, "the first time I ever went out to do missions, I had a fifty and two twenties in my pocket so I could use to buy the homeless breakfast and buy coats, gloves, whatever was needed.

"I went the whole day ministering with J.O.Y. but I never ran out of money. I just kept reaching in my pocket and there was always cash there. I never ran out. I just stepped out in faith and allowed the Lord to use me as I went along. It was a miracle!"

Claire gaped. Seriously? "That's amazing, Sister Rita! Wow. I don't even know what to say."

Rita shrugged sheepishly and smiled. "That is my little miracle. I have always heard of miracles happening to others but when a miracle happens to you there is no way for you to deny his presence and power. Now! On with the tour!" And with a little laugh, she pointed down the hallway.

"Slavery is back with force and brutality. This little room once held an ATM machine over here. Johns would be able to withdrawal money here with no fear. Each receipt would have a different business listing. Bob's Golf Supply. Whatever."

Turning behind her and pointing to part of the wall, she sighed, pain so evident in her brown wide set eyes.

"There once was a window here. The girls would stand on the other side of this wall. Showing only their faces."

Claire's heart thudded. It was as if this place almost had an intricate part in the dreams she was having. Icy fingers of fear tickled through her chest. She could almost hear the frantic murmuring of the girls' terrified voices. Different accents and languages, all panicked. Sweaty grasps of each other's palms for reassurance, anything that might help for the moment as their hearts flurried with panic..

Rita walked down the narrow hallway. "If you will follow me, I'll show you what once was the communal shower."

Claire looked at the cleaned and repainted shower blocks of cement. She imagined what they might have looked like full of murky slime.

"Sometimes there would be requests for a couple of girls to shower with them. The girls made the johns shower to keep police out. By law, Houston Police Department is not allowed to get naked on duty. This would prevent a raid from happening here."

Claire shook her head in disbelief. What a sick dark world.

"Over a matter of months we sent in men who have conversations on record stating that the owner knew about the prostitution. This originally was a massage parlor. In fact, prostitution funded the whole massage parlor and the owner was well aware of that. When presented with the information, he turned the deed over to us. We own this building now. Therefore, we are in the process of transforming this once hell-hole into a prayer room and a place of relief. Women can come here and shower, clean up, get a hot meal and find the love of Jesus. They can find help on their level."

"That's wonderful! And have you seen results?"

Daria cackled, "Oh, yes! We have a staff of about five women including your old friend, Shana Keni from the church downtown that work here and several others from the community as well. There ain't anything more compelling than seeing the light come back into a woman's eyes after a life of exploitation. Through our restoration work, we have had the incredible privilege of seeing this happen over the months of caring for these women."

Clair turned to stare at the smug little woman beside her. "Daria, you never told me about this place. It's unreal. I cannot believe y'all have control of the building now. Wow!"

"See what the Lord can do?" Daria laughed, "Working with these ladies has been the most rewarding thing in my life. God's love and favor toward us is not determined by who we are but by who He is! This is an answer to our prayers. And you are just in time, Claire! Just in time to be a part of His work!"

Rita leaned in as if to tell a secret. "When we are completely finished with this building, we will name it Nehemiah's Wall. Go read that book in the Bible. That book is filled with how to deal with spiritual warfare. Nehemiah rebuilt Jerusalem's walls with a building tool in one hand and a weapon in the other. He brought their children back home out of slavery and stayed encouraged. We will rebuild America's walls. We will free Houston's captives and with the Lord's help, we will utterly get rid of sexual slavery, in Jesus' name. This building will be named and anointed Nehemiah's Wall."

Claire was thoughtful for a moment as she began to take off the blinders and open her eyes. Maybe her dreams were not only of just one girl, Morgan Ann Bishop, but maybe the dreams represented many girls. Girls locked in slavery, crying out for help. Looking for a voice. Looking, praying for anyone who would be willing to speak out for them. Nehemiah's Wall. She liked it. She liked it a lot.

"Claire, this is my favorite room out of the whole building. Our war room. Our prayer room," Daria said over her shoulder as she opened one final door at the very end of the hallway. A young girl whom Claire could only assume was Azalea was kneeling at a folding chair praying.

Walking quietly inside, Claire noticed the small windowless room was almost completely empty aside from folding chairs and posters with the human trafficking hotline number and other statistics about human trafficking. Along the back wall hung another poster titled Interstate 10 Prayer guide.

"There are so many things I could be doing, Claire, but I spend most of my time here," Daria said humbly. I do most of my work on my knees in prayer. I am busiest in this room. There are so many areas in Houston we can be praying for. I choose to pray specifically for our ports.

"A barge can hold as much as fifteen tons of cargo. Not all containers can be inspected. I pray that port workers become educated on human trafficking, look for suspicious containers, and that resources and technology become available to make it possible to inspect more containers."

"Daria, I am so impressed. I had no idea," Claire said.

"We have ladies who come here to pray for specific areas that God lays on their hearts. Truck stops, motels, rest areas. They are all hot spots that need the angels of God to walk through."

"Claire," Rita said, "I want you to take this with you. This is basically the same thing you see posted on the wall, but this you can keep in your Bible to read and pray over." Rita handed Claire a stapled packet of pages.

"Thank you, Sister Rita." Claire smiled as she looked over the Interstate 10 prayer guide. Her eyes went to a bulleted list of prayer needs on the front page.

Pray that law enforcement along the I-10 corridor will be trained on what to look for.

Pray for the safety of our police.

Pray that the traffickers will be caught and prosecuted.

Pray that buyers will get caught and prosecuted.

Pray for buying to stop, so there would be no selling.

Knowing that God's grace is for everyone, pray for the trafficker and the buyer to be convicted of their sins and that they come to a saving knowledge of Jesus Christ, receiving the Holy Ghost. This does not mean that they should go free and not pay for the consequences of their crimes.

Pray for church ministries along the I-10 corridor as they seek to assist through providing shelter, food, clothing, transportation, and restoration.

Pray for churches along I-10 that they will become knowledgeable about human trafficking, be willing to educate others, and be open to minister where God leads.

Pray that billboards with information regarding trafficking and the hotline number will be placed along the I-10 corridor.

Pray that human trafficking is stopped on I-10.

Claire could hardly believe what she was seeing around her, and the prayers that were going forward to stop such evil in the world.

"Claire, when I stand before God at the end of my life, I want to be able to tell Him that I have not one drop of talent left. I want to tell Him that I used everything He gave me to use."

Claire nodded. She suddenly remembered what Pastor Manguia had said at church the other night. She could hear his voice in the back of her mind. *Do not allow Satan, your enemy, to shroud you in doubts and memories of past failures.*

She wanted to face her fear and stand up for what was right. She wanted to get involved. Nehemiah's Wall was an open door for ministry. The Lord was opening her eyes to a world she thought only existed overseas.

Kissing her favorite friend in the whole world on the cheek, Claire smiled at Daria. "I am so proud to know you. Really! Thank you for showing me this. I want to get involved! Ladies, thank you so much. I love everything you have done. I am so glad that you all took the time to show this to me."

Checking her phone, Claire noticed the time and ordered an Uber through her app to take her back to work. Cole would be getting off work and meeting her at her apartment soon.

"I gotta go. Cole said he had a surprise for me."

A mischievous twinkle appeared in Daria's eyes as she shooed Claire out the door.

"Thank you for coming by, sha. Now, go on! Cole can't be kept waitin'! By the way, church starts at seven tonight if y'all ain't busy!"

Pulling her old Fiat into her narrow driveway in front of the apartment, she saw Cole standing on her doorstep with a bouquet of white roses. She smiled as she saw his handsome face. He was dressed in his black uniform, which looked oh so dashing with his black hair.

Jumping out of the Fiat, she tried to appear much more casual than her skittering heart felt.

"Hi, Love. How are you?" Claire said stretching up on her tiptoes to plant a soft kiss on his chin, while taking the gorgeous roses from him.

Cole tenderly traced Claire's jawline and gazed into her eyes.

"I'm good now that I see you. You're so beautiful. Want to go to church tonight?"

"Thank you. Of course I do. I'm so glad you asked."

"I know work has gotten the majority of our time right now, but I want you to know that I love you so much. I am so glad we experienced what we did at church the other night. I want us to go back."

Claire smiled up into his dark, handsome eyes, nodding yes.

"Me too. I love you too. You are my safe haven. And I am glad we have a church to go to and be a part of now."

"Me too. I love you too." Cole stepped back and cleared his throat. "With that said, I really want to show you something."

Puzzled, Claire frowned, but with an excited giggle she took his arm. "Okay, what is it?

"A ring? His grandmother's perhaps?" she thought.

"It is actually just across the street," Cole said sheepishly running his fingers through his hair. "Turn around, Claire."

The sun was setting behind the lofty, brick townhouses that lined the street. All she could see was the tiny Fiat in the driveway and a large glittering SUV on the other side of the street.

"That sweet SUV you are looking at is yours. That is a Denali luxury SUV. White Diamond finish. It is a Yukon XL Denali, side blind zone alerts, V-8 engine. It has over 460 pounds of torque . . ."

Claire tuned him out as she stared at the gorgeous vehicle. She had driven the little Fiat so long; this new thing was an enormous monster, a gorgeous white diamond monster.

"Oh, wow, Cole! You did not! Unbelievable! Thank you so much!" Claire squealed. Whooping, she jumped in his arms and sprinkled his face with kisses.

Laughing, Cole hugged her tight.

"I thought you deserved this. Now, c'mon. I want you to see the leather interior. Plenty of room for a family one day."

Claire smiled at that thought. Cole would be a wonderful father, full of integrity and grace. They would make beautiful children together.

"You just wait until I see Daria! That sneak! She never let on that she knew at all."

"Good, I told her not to. She went with me to pick it out for you. This was one big secret. We have been together a long time, Claire. I knew the moment I saw you at that Bible quiz tournament that I wanted to spend the rest of my life with you. I love you more deeply today than last year, or even all those years ago."

Claire swallowed back her tears as she smiled up at Cole. What did she ever do to deserve such a wonderful man?

"Thank you so much. I love it. I love you!"

Cole tossed her the key as they crossed the quiet street. "Now you can see how this baby runs. Climb in."

CHAPTER 12

"When we are powerless to do a thing, it is a great joy that we can come and step inside the ability of Jesus."

—Corrie ten Boom

As they arrived at the church, Claire giggled as she tried to park the huge, new Denali. It was so much bigger than her Fiat. She would definitely have to get used to the wider frame.

Cole closed his eyes and muttered a half-joking prayer that Claire would not sideswipe any of the cars parked in the tiny parking lot.

"Maybe this wasn't the right size to buy for you," he said.

"No, it was! I love it," Claire retorted. "Hey, look there's Richard and Josie. Let's find a seat near them," Claire said nodding toward the front doors of the church. Their friends waved at them from the sidewalk outside the front door.

"Hey, Claire! Cole! I am so glad y'all are back," Josie gushed giving them both big hugs.

"Richard." Cole reached out to shake the man's hand.

"Cole. Good to see you, man." Richard's quizzical eyes turned to Claire. "How are you feeling? Sleeping any better?"

"I am, really. Thank you," Claire reassured him. Her smile was brighter and braver than her heart.

"Good. We have all been praying for you."

"Thank you. I appreciate that." Claire responded, so grateful for the amazing friends God put in her life.

"I'm singing up front in the choir today, Claire!" Josie announced, her gorgeous curls bouncing as she swung open the door to the small store front church with excitement.

"I can't wait to hear you! I am so happy to be here, Josie."

The keyboard was already beginning to play as Claire and Cole followed Richard into a row of folding chairs. Each one bowed their head to pray before the service began.

Moments later, Pastor Manguia greeted the congregation and asked the choir to lead the church in worship. It had been years since Claire had heard a choir sing. She was excited as she watched a small group of people began to sing. Josie fit right in.

The music began and the song's title and author displayed on a projection screen, which hung behind the pulpit. It read, *In Jesus' Name, by Darlene Zschech.*

As the choir started to sing, the music stirred Claire's soul. She focused on the words as they appeared on the screen. It was a powerful song and Claire allowed it to sink deep into her spirit.

> God is fighting for us
> Pushing back the darkness
> Lighting up the Kingdom
> That cannot be shaken
> In the Name of Jesus
> Enemies defeated
> And we will shout it out
> Shout it out
> I will live, I will not die
> The resurrection power of Christ
> Alive in me and I am free
> In Jesus' Name
> I will live, I will not die
> I will declare and lift You high
> Christ revealed and I am healed
> In Jesus' Name
> In Jesus' Name

Goosebumps spread all over Claire's body as the hair on her arms stood up in response to what she was feeling. It was not just a feeling, though. It was a force that seemed stronger than electricity, and so energizing. She knew she was in the presence of God.

Claire could see the church's prayer warriors already in the altar area worshiping the Lord. Daria was there praying as well. One hand rested heavily on her cane, but the other hand was raised in awe and wonder as she praised her Lord and Savior.

"Lord, open my eyes, that I might see you like they see you," Claire prayed. "Lord, I too want to be intimate and feel your presence and know your voice."

She closed her eyes tightly, trying to hold in her desperate tears. She wanted Jesus to be her Everlasting Father, the one to fill the empty place in her heart, the place where her father, Judge Sullivan, used to be. She hoped God would push away all of the fear and terror that tormented her at night. God was the only One powerful enough to push back the darkness from her life.

A breeze of the Holy Spirit seemed to blow through the small store-front church as the choir sang the song once more. People all around Claire began to speak in tongues and rejoice in the Spirit.

Open your eyes, child, and see the glory of the Lord. You have nothing to fear. You have no reason to faint, for the Lord God fights your battles.

The words were so clear, they seemed nearly audible. Claire knew in a heartbeat Who was speaking to her soul; it was Jesus. She carefully opened her eyes. When she looked around it was as if she were in an entirely different room than before. Now the room was completely full, not only with people, but she could see angels towering over the saints.

Claire's heart sped up as she glanced down at the altar where the people stood worshiping. The tallest angels were there, clad in warrior metals with spears and swords, and towering over eight feet tall. Two angels stood at attention behind the frail humans, Nina and Tina Nobles.

Shana Keni also had a massive commander angel that stood at attention behind her. They were beautiful creatures with strong wings, arms, and hands. Claire was afraid to look at their faces. She was in awe at the frailty of the little elderly twins compared to the gigantic angels that stood at attention during their bold prayers to the Father.

Claire closed her eyes, overwhelmed by what she thought she saw. Suddenly, she heard God's voice speaking to her again.

I am the Commander of angel armies. Trust in me. I will send my angels to guard over you, and to do my work in the spirit. You can win mighty battles in prayer by releasing your faith in me. Be the voice that frees the captives.

Claire's knees went weak. She was oblivious to whatever else was happening around her. All she knew was the she was in the presence of God. The church was entering into a Spirit-realm, as if heaven had come down to earth.

When she opened her eyes again, the angels were nowhere to be seen, but she knew they were there, and there was no doubt in her mind that spiritual warfare was real.

The worship and praise continued for several more minutes before the people returned to their seats and Pastor Manguia opened his Bible and began to speak.

"The Lord is truly pleased with our praise tonight. No power in hell can stop you when you have the attention of the Lord. When we begin to truly pray, the Spirit helps us fight our battles. Who better to help you than the Spirit of God, the One in charge? We can't overcome sin without the Him, but we can do all things through Christ who strengthens us."

Claire listened. She wanted to learn how to engage in prayer and spiritual warfare to moved heaven the way these people did.

The following week at work, Claire was distracted. She kept following up with Cole about Morgan Ann's case, but there were no new leads.

Every night, the nightmares would wake her up in cold sweats. When she woke up in the night, she would go into her living room and open up her Bible to read it aloud. She read the book of Nehemiah, as Daria and Rita had asked her to, as well as several comforting Psalms. Then she began to pray for Morgan Ann Bishop and all of the other children who were lost.

On her lunch break, Claire continued to read and take notes on the book of Nehemiah. She was a few chapters into the story when she received a phone call on her direct office line. The voice on the other line was very distinct; it was Shana Keni.

"Claire, I was thinking of you today and the Lord impressed upon me to give you a call."

"Hi, Sister Shana! How is it going down at Nehemiah's Wall? I was just thinking about all the great testimonies Daria and Rita were telling me last week, and I was reading in Nehemiah."

"Yes, things are going well. Thank you for asking. Read that book in the Bible. You will learn so much about spiritual warfare from it. Now, I have much to tell you." With no further hesitation, Shana launched into exactly why the Lord had her call Claire. She began to prophesy.

"Claire, thus saith the Lord: draw yourself unto Me, close to My side, and I will take you places you never dreamed of. I cannot use you to build My kingdom if you stay far away. You must act now, Claire. Fight against the merchants of innocent souls. Be My hands and feet. Let your light so shine before all men . . ."

Before Claire had the chance to respond, Sister Shana Keni had hung up the phone. All Claire could do was take one last determined breath and reach for her purse. She knew exactly what the Lord wanted her to do. She had felt it all morning. This phone call was a confirmation of what she had been feeling in prayer.

She had no time to retreat within herself or allow doubt or fear to weaken her. She had no time to be a wimp. She had no time to scare herself out of what God wanted her to do. She felt strength enter her body as she began to stand up against fear and anxiety.

A November breeze pushed her along as she walked across the lawn. With a firm step and one last straightening of her plaid skirt, Claire pushed open the door to the Human Resources office. The wind at her back seemed to edging her on encouragingly.

Quickly trying to remember the receptionist's name, Claire smiled vaguely at the blond-haired woman filing her nails at the desk. All she could remember was two years ago at the company Christmas party when the woman had flung herself all over Cole.

Lupyan. Bonnie Lupyan! Yes, that was her name.

Bonnie grinned at Claire, popping her pink bubble gum. "Hiya, Ms. Sullivan. What can I do's for ya?" Her accent sounded like she was from New Jersey.

"Good morning, Bonnie. I am applying for a personal leave of absence. I need to sign all the paperwork for approval please."

"What? Really?" smacked Bonnie. Her curiosity piqued. "Are you and that handsome hunk of yours getting hitched or something?"

Clenching her teeth, Claire tried to smile as she thought of Bonnie ever eying her "hunk" of a guy.

"No. Not yet. We are just waiting for the right time. It's just some personal business I need to take care of. Four weeks off of work would help out tremendously."

"So you're not pregnant?" Bonnie asked disappointedly. Her dyed blonde curls bouncing with each shake of her head.

"No, Bonnie. I'm not. If I were pregnant I would have come here requesting a maternity leave," Claire said, digging her nails into the palms of her hands trying to maintain her cool.

"Oh, right." Bonnie stood up, tugged her miniskirt down, and wobbled on her stilettos to gather the printed paperwork Claire would need to sign. Bonnie's shoulders seemed to slump from Claire's lack of juicy details.

Claire almost felt sorry for the woman, but then she remembered the Christmas party.

After gathering the pages she needed, Bonnie returned to her desk. "Just read these and sign," Bonnie said handing the packet to Claire.

Claire signed each page, filling in the required information. As soon as she handed the pages back to Bonnie and set the pen down on the desk, a weight seemed to lift from her shoulders.

This is the right thing to do," Claire thought, genuinely smiling. "Thanks, Bonnie. I appreciate your help. By the way," Claire leaned close and began to whisper. "Did you know Judge Duncan is getting a divorce?"

Bonnie's eyes sparkled at the news. Her toothy smile back at Claire was worth it all. Everyone knew Judge Duncan was the youngest, richest judge in the county, and now an eligible bachelor.

Laughing, Claire shook her head and slipped out the door. Gossip was not her thing, but making Bonnie's day felt appropriate.

Having a four-week personal leave from work would allow her to focus completely on finding Josie's friend, Morgan Ann Bishop, and get through the holidays. Maybe, Claire would even let Josie spend the weekend with her. Maesters always liked having Josie around.

Walking up to her Denali, Claire noticed a shoe box perched on top of the SUV. "What's this? Another surprise from Cole?" She asked herself.

She reached for the box, pulled it off the roof, and opened the lid. She almost dropped the box when she saw what was inside.

Long locks of mousy brown hair lay inside the box.

Under the hair was a handwritten note. Claire fished out the paper, rumpling the hair.

In spiky, authoritative letters, the message burned into her mind. She could feel an evil demonic presence as she read the note aloud.

Tell your King to forget the Bishop or he'll lose his Queen.
Your Bishop is only a pawn.
She has been lost forever.
She has been delivered to dance for hell.
Do not come looking for her, or
hell's fury will be unleashed worse upon
you than it has been for her, Ms. Sullivan.

Morricone

CHAPTER 13

"I think anyone who opened their heart enough to love without restraint and subsequently were devastated by loss knows that in that moment you are forever changed; a part of you is no longer whole. Some will never again love with that level of abandon where life is perceived as innocent and the threat of loss seems implausible. Love and loss, therefore, are linked."

—Donna Lynn Hope

"Burning the midnight oil?" Cole asked gently as he threw his keys on the end table. Warm lamplight pooled onto the living room floor, casting soft shadows around the couple. Cole lightly kissed Claire's forehead as he began to massage her stiff shoulders.

Exhausted, Claire closed the last file she was reading. Manila folders were strewn about the table, and Maesters was sprawled on even more files, all in disarray across the floor.

"You just got off work? What time is it?" She asked stretching the ache from her tense back muscles. The fire she had built some hours ago was dwindling, almost extinguished, so surely it was later than she anticipated.

"It is almost midnight." Cole said as he strolled into the kitchen scrounge for remnants of Daria's cooking that might still be lurking in the fridge.

Claire held the photo of Morgan Ann in her hand as she followed Cole into the kitchen. "She was in a safe place. She had so much going for her if she would have just kept up with the counseling. She didn't have to fall in the cracks, you know?"

"Maybe that's why she and Josie hit it off so well. They were both in the foster system." Cole replied as he poured sweet tea into a tumbler.

Claire stifled a yawn and rubbed her burning eyes. All of the reading had made her contacts dry.

"Someone has her now. I am so afraid for her. So what we do know is she is prone to bulimia. She has been known to cut herself prior to being in this foster parent's home. She has already tried to run away from the foster family before. She is one of four foster kids and she has been in counseling for the past year. She wanted a job and her driver's license, like any typical girl her age."

Clearing his throat, Cole turned and took Claire's shoulders in his broad hands. "Listen, I need to talk to you. I know you have a lot on your plate. I am glad you have chosen to take the next few weeks off work, but I have talked to Joels and we believe that you should just stay out of this one. It was really Joels' idea, but I agree with him."

Honesty and tact were two of the qualities Claire had always admired about Cole, until now.

"Excuse me? That's absurd! I saw this girl in my dreams. Did you forget that? She's linked to me somehow. I am the one the maniac chose to contact first. This is the first clue we've had concerning Morgan Ann Bishop."

Cole nodded and took Claire's face gently into his hands. "I know, sweetheart. I did not forget the note and the box. That was crazy. Thank you for bringing it straight to the police department after you found it. That was the right thing to do. Let the police handle the case. The closer we get to this being solved, the more uneasy I am about you being involved. The more I've learned about Jackson Miller and Adolf's Lair, the more I am afraid for you. This case is not going to end pretty. I don't want you in harm's way."

"What are you afraid of?" Claire scoffed. "Jackson is just a skinny, little punk kid. Adolf's Lair is a strip club. Morgan Ann isn't at Adolf's Lair or with Jackson. And I'm just going through files, digging for a clue. By the way, God can handle this. He's got everything under control, remember?"

"I understand that, but the dreams you're having are taxing on your health. I worry for you. Especially now that we know Morricone is in on this, and knows who you are, where you are, what you drive, and probably where you live. I do not want you to get hurt!" Cole reached out and touched a strand of Claire's black hair that had loosened from her twisted chignon.

Claire shrugged his hand away. "Cole, I appreciate your concern. I really do. Thank you. But I think I need to visit Morgan Ann Bishop's foster family in the morning. I am pushing past the dreams through prayer. They haven't been effecting me the same way since we started going back to church. I can see Morgan Ann's nightmare coming to an end, and nothing bad is going to happen to me. Besides that, Joels sent a plainclothes policeman this evening, and he's parked down the street watching everyone that comes and goes from this place. Plus, I already had a security system installed years ago."

Claire picked up the picture of Morgan Ann Bishop and held it up close to Cole's handsome face. "Look at her. Why in the world would I be the one to see her in my dreams? I will not give up on her now. I am all she has. I will not turn my back on her. She is not a lost cause."

Taking a deep breath, Cole looked sad. "Claire, you're not all she has. She has the whole department aware of her situation. This is not a debate. I am telling you, after the shoe box of Bishop's hair that possibly came from this guy named Morricone, I cannot let you anywhere near this case. You are not a police officer. You are a lawyer, and a temporarily unemployed one at that. From what we have learned, this type of move is classic of Morricone. He is ruthless. We believe that he is the one over the international human trafficking ring in this area and we have not been able to catch him yet."

Claire slammed her hands on the marble bar top, startling Maesters awake. She narrowed her eyes, "If I have to go to the streets myself alone to look for Morgan Ann Bishop, I will. It has been weeks since she's been missing."

"Every detective, every beat cop, every last police officer in the precinct knows your face, Claire. They will not let you anywhere near the evidence we have found on her abduction. You cannot be stubborn about this. Jackson Miller is about to go on the run. He is nervous, and when he does run, he will take us to where we need him to lead us. Please, stay out of this. I love you."

Claire's fatigue disappeared. Anger and frustration washed over her spirit. She felt as if her hands were tied.

"Cole, I don't need the precinct. I don't need your evidence. I don't need Joels, or you worrying about me. I don't even need that sleepy cop at the end of the street watching over my apartment. If I have to walk door to door all over Sharpstown, or wherever else Morgan Ann might be hiding, so be it."

"You don't need me? Claire, whether I like it or not, they already staged the raid on Adolf's Lair! Joels set it up. Morgan Ann was not there. We already know a lot of underage prostitution is going on. What are you going to do about that without police help? But, you don't need me, right?"

He laughed callously, shocking Claire as he tossed his dish into the sink. The splintered shatter of broken china silenced the room.

"You don't need me?" He repeated the question. "Okay, if that's the way you want it to be, fine."

"Cole, I can't believe you are acting like this." Claire desperately wanted to remedy what she had just said. She could not remember the last time she and Cole argued.

"*What is happening to us? What was going on? I just want him to tell me everything is going to be okay,*" she thought.

Surely, things should be much simpler between them since they had started going back to church, and started praying again. Just a few days ago people had prayed and prophesied over them. They had just recommitted their lives back to God. Did any of that matter?

Claire stood and squared her shoulders. Over a half a foot shorter than Cole, she stared up into his face.

"I am telling you right now. If it is the last thing I ever try to accomplish, I will find Morgan Ann Bishop. I am putting my whole heart into solving this case. This is more than a case to me. I lost my father. I made promises to Josie. I will not lose either of those girls. I have a gut feeling Morgan Ann will not be found tonight in that raid."

Cole shook his head, "After all you have been through, the trauma, the loss, all the nightmares . . . the last thing you need to do right now is immerse yourself further into this world. This is one of those cases that will completely drain you. It is going to get ugly. I do not want to see you get hurt. What if it is your hair coming to me in a box next time?"

Claire could sense his exasperation. She sighed, taking in a deep breath. She gently placed her hand over Cole's lips. She could feel her heart breaking and tears running in unapologetic lines down her face.

"I love you," she sobbed. "I do. But I am going to see this to the end."

"I can't stop you?" Cole begged.

Claire shook her head sadly.

"Well, Love, when you pick a lost cause, you really commit." Cole gently let go of her hand and began to gather his things to leave.

Claire's head began to spin.

"Claire!" she thought to herself. *"What are you doing? Stop him! Do not let him leave. He just bought you a brand new Denali. For goodness' sake, apologize!"*

"Where are you going?" She asked.

Cole looked down quietly before speaking. "If I can't stop you from being foolish, you'll do this alone. I can't bear to see you put yourself into danger. I'm leaving."

With those gentle last words, Cole firmly opened the front door. Cold air swirled into the room whipping around Claire's ankles.

With one last disappointed look at the woman he loved, Cole retreated into the night.

CHAPTER 14

"And take my past and take my sins,
Like an empty sail takes the wind.
And heal, heal, heal, heal."

—Tom O'Dell

Claire's phone began to ring before the sun rose the next morning. Lyrics to one of her favorite songs played through her head as she reached for the phone.

"When you're dreaming with a broken heart, waking up is the hardest part."

"Hello?" Claire mumbled. The caller ID told her it was Daria who was calling.

"Pastor Manguia called for a early mornin' prayer meetin' and I want you to take me."

"What time is it, Daria? I have to meet Misti later for lunch. I really just want to sleep in."

"Sorry, child, but I need ya. I am at the front door. The policeman who watches out for ya at night is here with me. He won't let me in. Come see. Open up."

Groaning, Claire added firing the police officer to her day's to-do list. Tripping over Maesters who was asleep at her bedroom door, Claire grabbed her glasses off her bookshelf and stumbled down the hallway to the front door.

Claire glared out at the officer and Daria.

"Seriously, dude? She's an old lady . . ."

"Who you callin' old?" Daria butted in.

"What is she going to do?" Claire continued without missing a beat. "Hit me over the head with her cane? Come on in, Daria."

"Just doing my job, lady," the young policeman said as Claire slammed the door in his face.

"Daria, did you try to call Cole yet? Did you storm into his apartment? Did you ask him to get up and go to prayer?" Claire complained, securing her bathrobe belt as she made her way to the kitchen.

Daria was already scooping coffee into the filter. "No, I didn't, but I guess I should've. What's going on, Claire? Sister Avis Wheeler dropped me off. I thought you'd want to go to the church with me. You know I don't like to drive in the fog."

Daria reached down to pet Maesters who had just waddled into the kitchen sniffing for his breakfast.

"Do not make me feel guilty, Daria. I am tired. I have to meet Misti later. I will take you to church. I just did not want to go and see Cole if he was going to be there."

"Sheep and doves, Claire, not wolves and serpents. You got to be kind. What's going on with you and him anyway?"

Claire rehearsed the previous night's events to Daria, trying hard not to cry.

"You two are meant to be together, Claire. This is the work of the devil trying to split you two up. You just need to learn to submit to that man if he ever gonna be your husband," Daria said, spooning sugar into her fresh, hot cup of coffee.

"Fine. Let me get dressed and I will take you to church."

"You better hurry, honey. I don't like to be late and someone take my seat."

Claire smiled at the older woman's spunk. Reluctantly, she headed back to her room to dress. As she walked, she felt a tremendous amount of shame and condemnation flood her soul. The Lord had rescued her from the guilt and sin that was in her life. The least she could do was enter into His presence with a thankful heart, regardless of the hour, or of the state of her relationship with Cole.

An hour later, Claire pulled the Denali into the church parking lot, and she and Daria walked toward the storefront. As they entered into the sanctuary, Daria scowled.

Claire knew her all too well; the displeasure came from two sources: Avis Wheeler was sitting in Daria's spot, and Reverend Manguia was already exhorting. Claire had them running a little late, if eight in the morning could be classified as "late." Despite it all, she still felt the presence of the Lord.

Daria marched on up the middle aisle to scoot Avis Wheeler down the row and take her seat back. Claire slid into a chair near the back, next to Shana Keni who handed her a Bible as Reverend Manguia continued sharing his heart.

"I feel an urgency to share certain scriptures the Lord impressed on my heart with you all," the pastor said. "I want to begin by announcing that we will have morning prayer every day for the next several weeks. I feel a tug of the Spirit to usher us into a new dimension. A dimension of becoming the prayer warriors that the Lord asked us to be.

"The Holy Spirit is taking us into a new dimension, to pull down strongholds and spiritual wickedness in high places in Jesus' Name; however, that takes us fully giving ourselves over to God. I was reading in my Bible last night, Deuteronomy 15:12-17, and God spoke a message into my spirit that I have to share."

He read the passage, and then slowly began to speak.

"As I was studying for this message, I learned the slavery which existed among the ancient Jews was a very different thing from that which disgraces humanity in modern times. Can you imagine being a slave that loved your master so much, that you volunteered to remain his slave for the rest of your life? Not only that, can you see yourself willingly go through a painful ceremony where a big nail was thrust through the bottom of your earlobe, marking you a voluntary slave for life?

"Then, God led me to Acts 9:1-9," Pastor Manguia continued, telling the story of young Saul.

The passage was very familiar to Claire, being that she was raised in church. She knew about Saul, the man who held the coats of people as they threw stones to kill the first martyr, Stephen.

She listened intently as Pastor Manguia read the Bible passage that told of Saul's Damascus Road conversion. One encounter with Jesus set Saul free, transformed him into Paul, and empowered him to turn the world upside down.

"The Lord laid these passages of scripture upon my heart last night," Pastor Manguia explained, "and I stayed awake pondering their meaning until I believe the Lord gave me an explanation. From the beginning, Saul—the Apostle Paul—in his heart of hearts, wanted to please the Lord. He thought he was doing the work of the Lord by persecuting people who were against the one true God.

"When Jesus knocked him off his horse and blinded him that day on the road to Damascus, Saul had a date with destiny. He was destined to become a love-slave to the Lord Jesus Christ, one who would serve the Lord with all of his being and would find his identity in Jesus Christ alone."

Claire was intrigued. She had heard both stories before, but had never put them together. She searched for a pen and paper in her purse to jot down some notes as Reverend Manguia continued.

"In my studying, I came across a thought by Spurgeon about being a servant either to sin or to Christ. He wrote:

"If you are resolved to be the slave of your passions, then your passions will, indeed, enslave you; if you are content to be a slave of the cup, you shall find that the cup will hold you by its fascinations as fast as captive in fetters of brass; if you are willing to be the slave of unbelief and of the pleasures of the flesh, you will find that they will fasten you as with bands of steel, and hold you down forever!

"There are times when men might get free; their prison door is, for the moment, on the latch. Many others in the same condition have been all but free—but they have deliberately preferred to remain as they were, and the result has been that sin has bored their ear, and from that day forward they have seldom been troubled by conscience!

"Let that sink in for a moment. Go back over the words I just spoke into your hearing and truly think about them." Pastor Manguia paused for a moment of silence.

"You have a choice here today. You can choose to be a slave to sin, or to God. Being a servant of God is an honor. God spoke of Abraham as His servant. Joshua is called the servant of the Lord, as was David and Isaiah. In all of these instances, the term servant carries the idea of humble nobility.

"Jesus taught that the greatest in God's kingdom would have to become the servant of all. As bond-servants to Christ, we renounce other masters and give ourselves totally to Him. What we get in return is eternal life with Jesus Christ our Lord, and we receive the power to push back the darkness in our world!"

Amens resounded through the house as Reverend Manguia asked everyone find a place to pray for their city. People went to stand along each wall in the church, believing in faith for Jesus to save lost souls from the north, south, east, and west parts of the city.

Claire knelt at her chair, tears flowing from her full heart. She was ready to follow Jesus anywhere He led her, regardless of any nightmare that might haunt her. She would do what the Lord asked her to do, and she knew exactly what that was.

Finding Morgan Ann was Claire's mission from God, but it did not stop there. God was calling her to fight modern day slavery by becoming a love slave to Jesus Christ and pushing back the darkness of their city through the power and light of the Holy Spirit.

CHAPTER 15

"Now is the time to awaken from our sleep, for our salvation is nearer now than when we first believed."

—Romans 13:11

Gorgeous, lithe, Misti Jacobs nibbled on her fresh cobb salad as she stared across the booth at Claire. "I caught Josie crying in the garage last night. She was busy making more pottery all weekend," she said.

Claire frowned. "Poor Josie. She's seriously worried about her friend, isn't she?"

Misti nodded as she took a sip of her kale, pineapple, and green apple concoction. "Richard has talked about starting her on antidepressants, but I just do not think that is the way to go. Those medications are too much. They really are unhealthy. And, Josie has her good moments, like singing in the church choir, where she is happy and distracted for a while."

Claire sighed and quit picking at her fish tacos. "What other choice to you have, Misti?"

Frustrated, Misti just shook her head. "I've been thinking. Josie is going with the church youth group to a concert in Katy this weekend. After that, I am taking her to Galveston and renting a beach house for the winter. I will homeschool her for a semester, and Richard can come down on the weekends."

Seeing Claire's shocked reaction, Misti held up her hand. "Wait! Before you even say anything, I have already talked to Pastor Manguia about it. There is a church we can attend in Galveston, so it isn't as if we will be totally isolated. The change of scenery will do us good."

"How long have you thought about this?" Claire asked.

"Long enough that I have made my decision. I just didn't know how to tell you. I think this really is the best thing I can do for Josie."

"What? Run? That's your plan?" An incredible sadness cloaked Claire as she tried hard to fight back her tears. Evil monsters took away her father, Cole was gone, insane lunatics somehow took Morgan Ann, and fear and depression was taking her best friend away for a while.

Despite her objections, in the deepest part of her heart she knew it was for the best that they go away for a while

Claire thought about the prayer meeting that morning. God called her to do her part to fight against human trafficking and sex slavery, but that was her calling—not Misti's calling or Josie's. As much as she did not want to be alone in her obedience, she knew God created her for a purpose and the price she had to pay was hers alone, and not for her to force on anyone else.

"Misti, you know I want you and Josie to stay nearby. I don't want you to go and I am going to miss being able to see you both whenever I want, but . . ."

Claire still had not told Misti about the letter and the locks of hair she received yesterday. She did not want to scare her even more, but she had to be honest about it, for all of their safety.

"When I went out to the Denali after work yesterday, someone had left a note for me at my car. We know traffickers have Morgan Ann," she said, sparing the morbid details about the locks of hair. "I don't want to scare you, but I think it is good for you go. Maybe you should leave even sooner than you're planning."

Claire shared the details of what the letter said, and what Cole had told her about Morricone. There was still no specific clues about where to find Morgan Ann Bishop. Police had arrested several people involved with trafficking, but none connected to her case. That could only mean one frustrating thing: the raid had clearly not helped. It only sent the kidnappers deeper into hiding, and kept Josie, and everyone else connected, at risk.

With sad, gray eyes, Misti shook her head in disbelief. "Claire, what if this guy, Morricone, or whatever his name is, comes back?

This is not a normal situation, is it? Something bad happened. Before you even got the letter, you said it was possible that someone kidnapped Morgan Ann. And now we know you were right. I can't risk losing Josie. She needs to get away. I've made up my mind; we will leave tonight."

Frustrated, Claire knew she could do nothing to solve her immediate loneliness problem. "We aren't going to be able to spend Thanksgiving together like normal," Claire said sadly.

Misti rolled her eyes sarcastically. "Oh, dear. I know how sad you'll be not eating my tofu dressing this year."

That thought brought a bittersweet smile to Claire's face. It would be the first year in a long time she had not spent her favorite holiday with her best friends. "Well, Galveston isn't too far away, I guess I could handle Thanksgiving on the beach."

The waiter dropped the lunch bill on the table and Misti scooped it up before Claire had the chance to grab it.

"I'm paying! No protesting," Misti said. "Take it as a thank you from me to you, for being my best friend. You are always there for me, and even though you are sad, you understand why I have to leave, and you support me. Thank you. Thank you so much for being selfless, searching for Morgan Ann, and making Josie a priority."

With that, Misti stood up, smoothed the front of her black and white chevron skirt, gave her friend a hug, and headed to the cash register.

No longer able to hold back her hot tears, Claire picked up her napkin and wiped her eyes. Her whole world was falling apart, bit by bit. How many more losses would she have to endure before those demonic people were caught?

A moment of strength came and Claire made up her mind that crying was not going to do any good. Regardless of what Cole said, she was going back to Sharpstown. She was going to talk to Jackson—Morgan Ann's boyfriend—one way or another. But first, she had a foster family to visit.

When was the last time anyone had reached out to the foster family? What was their last name? Claire mentally shuffled through all the information she had learned about the case. There were three other children in the home—elementary school aged boys.

"Bertrand! That is it! Dylan and Susan Bertrand. They had been a foster family for over five years, and Morgan Ann had lived with the family for over a year." Claire's mind began to race with information.

Grabbing her keys, she headed for the door. Claire climbed into the Denali, thumbed through the case files she had stashed under the passenger seat, and found the Bertrand's address, which she quickly entered into her GPS.

It did not dawn on her exactly where the family lived until she began to drive down the diminishing neighborhood streets into the Fifth Ward.

The Fifth Ward looked tired, done with holding up a façade. People no longer wore fake smiles or attempted to greet each other. It was as if the theoretical rug that all of the dirt was once swept under was pulled out from under Houston's feet, exposing it for the whole world to see. Worn out, brick, cookie-cutter government housing sagged along the potholed streets. Forgotten people drowned in Fifth Ward misery, lost in the cracks.

"Was anyone doing anything at all about the children that lived here?" Claire thought as she slowed to read the house numbers painted on the curb. As she drove past each dilapidated house, she counted at least a dozen toddlers playing on faded-plastic trikes, and swing-sets that were missing half the swings. Exhausted mothers barely noticed the huge Denali as Claire slowly passed by.

She finally arrived at the corner lot on Goleman Avenue and Perry Street. Two rusty bikes stood guard along a broken concrete driveway. The old carport sat empty. The lot's quietness made Claire feel uneasy.

There was no comforting, lovely features to make this house a home. In neighborhoods like this, there was no extra money to add thoughtful touches of care, no rose bushes, no seasonal pumpkins, or holiday decorations.

A stray calico cat quickly scampered across the yard as Claire stepped out into the bitter November wind. Black iron bars on the windows and doors of each house gave the entire street a prison type of feeling. This house was no exception.

"Do social workers even visit foster home anymore?" Claire thought in dismay. Before she even had a chance to knock on the door, a raspy voice of a chain-smoker called out from behind her.

"Whatcha' want, lady? You from social services? Comin' to badger our Susan again?"

Claire turned to see a skinny pocked-faced Caucasian lady with thinning red hair standing on the street by a scroungy wire-haired dog. She was probably younger than she looked, perhaps early forties, but life choices made her appear to be at least sixty. Claire stepped off the small porch and headed toward the woman.

"I am a lawyer. My name is Claire Sullivan. I am looking for Susan."

"Don't you think you people have harassed that poor girl long enough? Took all her kids away, then here you are again coming by, riding up in your fancy car asking more questions, taking more of them away . . ."

"Bobbie, stop!" A soft voice gently commanded from inside the now open door of the house. Claire had not heard the door open. Whirling around, she could make out a faint silhouette standing in the shadows.

"Susan?"

"Susan? Yeah, that's me. Come in." Then, a little louder, she called out beyond Claire to the woman. "Bobbie, you stay out of my business, you hear?"

The raggedy older woman shook her head in disgust and spit at Claire before making her way down the street.

"Come in. Don't mind her. She's just a cranky neighbor," Susan said, holding the screen door wide open.

"Well, thank you. I am Claire. Claire Sullivan, a lawyer at . . ."

"Doesn't matter much to me who you are. What do you want?" The mousy woman asked.

Now that Claire could see her better, she thought the woman looked like various shades of brown. Brown, beachy, leather skin, brown gravy clouded eyes, brown chestnut frizzy hair.

As Claire walked into the dark kitchen, her eyes began adjusting to the dim light. The kitchen smelled of bacon grease. A Houston Chronicle lay open, spread across a large, round, solid oak table. Surprisingly enough, the kitchen was completely clean. Breakfast dishes were washed and stacked drying. The strains of soft country music drifted in from a nearby room.

"What did you expect?" Susan asked cynically. "Crack pipes lying around? Week old trash spilling out, rotting on the floor? I am a foster mom, not a junkie. We did not always live in this neighborhood, you know."

Susan gathered up the newspaper and motioned for her to have a seat at the kitchen table.

"Dylan's grandfather made this table, you know. It is one of the only possessions Dylan held on to and would not sell during the recession some years back. We tried to keep up. We used to live in the Museum district, you know."

Claire intently watched the woman as she listened to her speak. Susan was a strong woman. A woman with great conviction in her voice. Claire felt ashamed for the silent judgments she projected onto the woman because of her surroundings.

Pouring herself a cup of coffee, Susan returned to the table and sat, deep in thought. "Our house foreclosed," she explained. "It was like we woke up one day, looked around, and everything was gone, everything, and we were here. All alone."

Claire was not sure what to say. She had arrived with a preconceived idea of what she would find, but each of those stereotypes dissolved before her eyes. Susan's house was so clean; though her pride was wounded, and her heart broken.

"Where are the children?" Claire ventured.

Tears welled up in the woman's eyes. Embarrassed, she stood and walked to the sink.

"You want a cup of coffee? I have Community dark roast. Dylan only drinks Community Coffee."

Declining, Claire waited for an answer to her question about the children.

Returning to her seat, Susan composed herself, took a deep breath and smiled.

"So that's why you are here. The kids are gone. Taken to other foster homes. Three boys. Malik, Samuel, and Jonathan. Dylan and I loved those boys."

Claire regretted not accepting the cup of coffee now. It would have given her something to attend to while Susan tried to gather her emotions about her.

"They were good kids, you know. Even Morgan Ann, as troubled as she was," Susan said, pointing her dark, somber eyes toward Claire.

"I believe you," Claire said tenderly. "That's why I'm here, to try to learn more about Morgan Ann. How many times had she run away prior to this last time, Susan? I am looking for her. I need to know what she was like."

After a brief pause, relief flashed through Susan's eyes. "She ran away at least twice before this time. Once was the first Christmas she came to us. She ran away Christmas Eve night. Malik was sleeping under the Christmas tree, waiting on Santa to come when he saw her take off out the front door." Susan's sad face brightened with a slight reminiscent smile.

"God, how I miss all those kids, you know. The last time . . . this time when Morgan Ann ran away, we thought we could find her. We looked for forty-eight hours before we went to the authorities, then the social workers started showing up. After the second time she ran away, social workers came to evaluate the home, the kids, and interview us. They said if Morgan Ann ran away again, we could lose all the kids. They said we were not being attentive enough, you know."

Claire nodded. She understood the system quite well.

"Dylan started taking Morgan Ann to school and picking her up after. We always kept her in our sight, always. Morgan Ann promised not to leave again. She cared about the boys, loved them, I think. But she was constantly looking, searching for something, someone, to fill the void in her heart. She wanted answers as to why she was the one thrown in a dumpster as a baby. She wanted to know why. That sense of abandonment never would leave her."

Susan wiped away her tears and drained the last of the coffee from her mug. "So we searched for her," she continued. "Dylan finally gave up, knowing we had really lost her this time. The next day, social workers were here for the boys. Malik screamed and cried not wanting to leave. I fed the boys blueberry pancakes and bacon and eggs that last morning."

Recounting that memory filled Susan's eyes to the brim with tears. Claire reached for her hand.

"They have all been gone for over a month now. All four of them. I pray for Morgan Ann and the boys every night. I stay by the phone, hoping she will call, but she never has. She was always such a resentful child. She's been in foster care all her life, you know. Never had a real family for long."

Susan's tears overflowed at this point, falling onto the table and into her empty coffee mug. "So that's why you came, huh? For the story?"

"Yes, I guess so. Honestly, this was not what I expected."

"No one ever does, you know."

"I don't really know what to say. I know there is nothing I can say to take away the pain."

"I'm not angry, Ms. Sullivan. I am not like Bobbie on the street. I knew I would lose those kids eventually. Morgan Ann is a wandering soul. One of the boys was able to go back to his family. CASA workers are still working with the other two boys. Because it's what the boys want, I get to visit them once a week for an hour or so. You know, I used to tell my kids all the time that I believe in the sun, even when it is not shining. I believe in God, even when He is silent, and I believe in love, even when I am all alone."

Claire smiled at Susan's resilience.

"Susan, I am so sorry." She paused for a moment before turning the conversation back to Morgan Ann. "Did you know that Morgan Ann had a boyfriend?"

"I had no idea. The kids at school would not talk to Dylan or me. Not to the police, to no one. Misti Jacobs was the only one who opened up to me and told me about how Josie was Morgan Ann's best friend at school."

Claire nodded her head. Susan did not know about Jackson Miller. Feeling obligated, Claire told the poor woman everything she knew about Jackson and how Morgan Ann most likely ran away to be with him.

By the time, Claire finished, Susan had doubled over on the oak table sobbing. After a few minutes, she leaned back and took in a deep breath.

"Thank you, Ms. Sullivan. Thank you for telling me. Can you just see yourself out? I need time to think, you know."

"Susan, I want to pray with you before I go." Claire said softly once again reaching for her hand. "Jesus, thank You for allowing me to meet this wonderful woman. She has attended to Your work. She is constantly thinking of and caring for Your children. I ask you to give her comfort and peace. Bring her babies back home if it is Your will. In Jesus name, I pray. Amen."

With a quick squeeze of her hand, Claire let go of Susan's hand and showed herself out of the house into the brilliant sunshine. Somehow, she felt older and wiser.

She saw the street a little differently this time. She noticed an older woman sweeping off her porch. The woman may not have had seasonal decorations out, but her lawn was clean. She saw a man run to help catch a neighbor's dog that had escaped from his leash.

Claire felt a sense of hope. She felt stronger inside, more settled, as she eased her Denali back out onto the road and into the city traffic. As she drove down the street, she watched a couple carrying an elderly man's groceries into his house while he leaned on his cane.

Claire's smile grew as she noticed each small act of kindness. Her faith expanded and her confidence in Christ's love consumed her. One small gesture may only seem like a drop in the ocean, but, one day, the tide would turn and the world would a better place for future generations.

CHAPTER 16

"And the light shined in darkness—shines even on fallen man—but the darkness—dark, sinful man—perceived it not."

—John 1:5, *Wesley's Notes on the Bible, Commentary*

Morning's fog clung like a shroud draping over Houston. Wisps of haunting clouds hugged the earth in one last dance before dawn clawed and fought back for its rightful territory. Light and dark met in the smoky haze.

Claire wanted to immerse herself into the fog, baptize herself in the imminent dewy shadows, washing away all thoughts of the things she had recently learned. How could she get up and go on with life, knowing what evil lurked on nearby streets?

How could society commute to work daily, blind to evil, oblivious to the underworld all around them? How could Claire have so much knowledge about the problems of her society, and yet be so powerless to do anything to change it?

She thought of the girls, the ones locked away, drugged, dependent, abused. The girls like Morgan Ann. Every pale morning's dawn reminded the slaves, the victim, and the women in chains that they were a day older and another day deeper, drowning in bondage.

Claire desperately needed help from the Lord and her church family. She did not want to turn into an insomniac, afraid of the future, afraid of the past, afraid of the tormenting darkness of worry. Misti and Josie were gone for now, safely tucked away in Galveston; hopefully out of harm's way. She needed to get out of herself, to connect to others, and to trust in God.

God was the only One who could lead the way for Claire to find Morgan Ann Bishop. He was the only One who could lift and carry the burden that weighed heavily on her shoulders. At times, the compassion she embodied for the many girls lost in the evil mix of slavery and trafficking would overcome her heart and emotions.

But today, she had a plan. She was going to confront Jackson Miller.

As she arrived at Jackson's apartment complex, Claire saw no sign of the police detail that was supposed to be watching the area. She shook away her thoughts as she climbed the rickety fire escape to Jackson's apartment.

Today would be the day everything changed. She was not leaving his apartment until she received an answer about Morgan Ann.

She remembered a historic tactic of a Native American Indian tribe that had once worked. They would storm their enemy's camp screaming. The screams would startle the enemy into a defense mode, and bring a swift victory to the attacking tribe. Claire decided that would be the best tactic for her to use on Jackson Miller.

Taking a deep breath, Claire charged through Jackson's unlocked apartment door. Barging into the musty, smoke-hazed room, she screamed at the top of her lungs.

"WHERE IS SHE?" Claire demanded as she kicked the side of the rundown couch. "WHERE IS SHE? WHAT DID YOU DO WITH HER?" Claire screamed into Jackson Miller's slack face. "WHAT HAVE YOU DONE WITH HER?" She yelled.

Jackson was in a drug-induced stupor. He had all the classic signs of an opioid overdose. He should not have woken up, even if vigorously shaken. God showed mercy on Claire as Jackson stirred.

"Lady, I dunno whatcha talkin' 'bout. Get outta my house, crazy witch." Jackson cursed, rolling over to his side on the flea-infested, filthy couch. Falling to the floor like a sack of potatoes, his head slumped forward, drool oozing out the corner of his protruding lips.

Claire knew she should call 911 to get Jackson some help, but Morgan Ann was more important to her. Desperately, she grabbed Jackson's shirt collar, shaking him until his heavy eyelids partially opened, revealing his pinpoint pupils. Insufficient oxygen in the blood caused his lips and fingernails to have a faint blue shade.

Claire only had a short amount of time to get him to talk. "Jackson, WAKE UP! Please, wake up! Where's Morgan Ann? Everyone knows she was here."

"Sold her, man." Jackson weakly tried to shove Claire's hands away. "Some crazies. Serbs. European dudes showed up. Offered me some of this stuff. The good drugs. Told me to stay away in exchange for Morgan Ann."

Blood rushed to Claire's head. She felt dizzy.

"What in the world was he telling her? He sold Morgan Ann for a hit? Sold her! Where could she be now?"

Claire's dreams came flashing back, mocking her. Morgan Ann was screaming. Staring at the wall. Bleeding. Claire's stomach felt sick.

"Cole was right. Morgan Ann is a victim of sex trafficking," she thought.

"Jackson! Who gave you the drugs? Who did this to you? Jackson, answer me, PLEASE!" With a rough kick to his groin, Claire woke him up once more.

"Some big dude . . . that's all. Came lookin' for Morgan . . ."

"Where is she now?" Surely, the girl had not been sold into a brothel for less than a couple of hundred dollars of drugs.

A stream of curses erupted from the boy. "Lady, I could care less. I don't need her no more. Let someone else use her now." And with that he was gone, lost in oblivion, the drugs completely taking over.

Disgusted, Claire felt like leaving him there to die. It would only be a few minutes and he would be gone forever. Dead and in hell where he belonged. Giving the lowlife one last hard kick, she reached into her pocket, and pulled out her phone to call an ambulance. The police had been watching Jackson's apartment for days. How could he have digressed this far?

"This is it. I have to find her," Claire thought.

The haunting whispers of demonic despair nibbled away at any hope Claire previously felt. She was supposed to rescue Morgan Ann.

"Too late. Too late," chanted the demons as they gleefully danced on her shoulders. *"You'll never find her now."*

"I have to find Cole," Claire thought as she raced down the filthy corridor. *"Oh, God, please help me to find Morgan Ann and Cole."*

"He's gone too. Gone. Gone. Gone. You're all alone," victorious whispers laughed in her ear as she slammed into the exit door and took the fire escape stairs two at a time. Stumbling through her tears, she fell as she ran to her Denali.

"So afraid. Oh, so afraid. Fear is your best friend, a warm blanket that will take you back into hiding." The spirit of fear tried to lure her.

"Oh, Cole, I need you. Oh, God, please let him pick up the phone," Claire prayed as she dialed his number. She put her keys into the ignition. Cole's phone sent her straight to voicemail.

"Cole, I'm so sorry. Please call me. Morgan Ann has been trafficked. You were right all along. This is a part of what you have been looking into. I love you. Call me. I was at Jackson's apartment."

An ambulance wildly screeched to the scene as Claire pulled her SUV away, completely unsure where she was headed. Who was she going to talk to? Maybe she could find someone downtown, like one of the women working the street. Maybe they would have seen a new young girl?

Claire wiped away her tears and grabbed her steering wheel. Determination and anger settled into her belly, when, suddenly, she felt a small, cold, metallic kiss on the side of her right temple.

The smell of icy-mint breath caressed her cheek. Someone was in the backseat of her Denali.

"You weren't paying much attention, *chica*."

Startled, Claire careened her vehicle up onto the edge of the sidewalk.

"Easy now, *chica*," the Hispanic male voice said as the man pressed the gun tighter against her skin.

What was the name Cole had said that night weeks ago? The name of the man in Cole's trafficking case file, was it Suarez? Alfonso Suarez? This must be one of Alfonso Suarez's coyotes.

Claire's fear was so overpowering, it felt as if her body was going to melt. What was he going to do to her? Claire eased her hand into the side pocket of the car door, searching for her can of mace or her Kubotan . . . anything to use as a weapon to defend herself.

"I don't think so, Ms. Sullivan. Hands where I can see them, NOW! You were looking for us. We decided to grant you your little wish, and pay you a visit."

Claire could barely breathe. This was all too real. She had been so stupid! Of course, they had followed her.

"Do not make me shoot you, *Hermosa*," the man threatened. "Pull over, put the car in park, and slide across to the passenger seat. I'm driving now."

Claire did as the man commanded, and moved to the other front seat. The man kept the gun on her head as he climbed into the driver's seat.

"We have an appointment to keep. Merchandise to see. And you, you, my dear are so much more beautiful in person." His thick accent and menacing tone sent chills down Claire's arms. "Morricone is requesting your presence."

Surely, he was not talking about the man Cole had been searching for so long? Did these powerful men really have the audacity to show their faces now, with so many cops after them?

"Don't even think about running, *chica*. Where we are headed are all abandoned buildings. No one will find you. No one will hear you scream. In fact, why don't I just help you out a little bit, so you can relax as I drive."

"NO! DON'T!" Claire reached to open the door and run, but the man was too strong. With a quick, vice-like grip, he pulled her hair, and held her head against the seat, smothering her with a cloth.

"Don't breath. Don't breath. Just fight. Claw him. That's right, Claire. Scratch and claw and kick and get away. Don't breathe it in. It takes at least five minutes of inhaling a rag soaked in chloroform to render a person unconscious. You can fight this crazy man off. Push away the darkness!"

"You are too predictable, Ms. Sullivan. Did you think I would let you claw my eyeballs out?" With a small pinch, Claire could feel the tiny prick of a needle stabbing her in the side of her neck, and she immediately began to feel dizzy.

"Diazepam, *chica*. That's the trick. That's good. Get still. You have an appointment. A dinner date, of sorts, later on. Shh, no worries. You will wake up later."

With one last silent, panicked prayer, and thoughts of Cole and Daria, Claire slumped against the passenger's side door as the darkness triumphed over her.

CHAPTER 17

"There's always a moment that separates the past from the future, and that moment is now."

—Aniekee Tochukwu Ezekiel

Groaning, Cole rubbed his hand across his unshaven face. His thoughts constantly returned to Claire, even at work when he should be focused.

Seeing Claire's number flash across the screen of his cell phone only made things worse. What did he have to say to her? He loved her so much, but needed to keep her at an arm's distance. She would be hurt if he told her what was going on with the case.

Decision made. He sadly pressed the decline button on the phone and stood up from his desk, heading to his car to pray. He knew there was power in prayer. He needed to tap into a supernatural level. He needed access to the throne room of God.

As he walked, his heart ached. He was so torn. He had made up his mind, but his heart was balking. He had to give himself some room to breathe, some hope for the future.

Cole promised himself he would propose to Claire after Morgan Ann's case closed. He needed Claire in his life. She completed him. The time they had spent apart recently made him realize even more how much he loved her.

In addition, he would get out of the police business. He was ready to lay his badge down and move on to God's work and calling on his life. Claire would understand. She just had to.

But first, Cole had to find Morgan Ann.

Cole was eating a late dinner at Huynh's with Daria. The older woman had just finished volunteering at Nehemiah's Wall, and called Cole to bring her home since it was nearing sunset and she hated to drive after dark.

Cole smirked at the lovely older woman. He secretly suspected she was not afraid to drive in the dark, but was just lonely and liked to have company. Either way, he never minded driving her home. She was like a grandmother to him. Surely, God had shaken his head the day he built her, but Cole bet everything that God had smiled. The strength and zeal that old Creole lady possessed was impressive.

"Daria, have you heard from Claire at all today?" Cole asked as pulled out his phone and dialed to check his voicemail.

After nodding for the server to take her plates, Daria looked at Cole and shook her head, "No. She went to prayer with me yesterday morning and mentioned she was goin' to visit Morgan Ann's foster family, but I ain't heard from her today. Have you?"

Now he felt the gnawing sense of guilt and regret. Distracted, Cole nodded. "She left me a message," he muttered as he tried to focus on the recording. A fist of fear squeezed his gut as he intently listened. He hung up on the message and tried to call Claire. Her number did not even ring; his call went directly to her messaging system. Frustrated, he hung up again, re-dialing his voicemail.

"Daria, listen to this!" Cole said, replaying the message on speaker for her to hear.

"Cole, I'm so sorry. Please call me. Morgan Ann has been trafficked. You were right all along. This is a part of what you have been looking into. I love you. Call me; I was at Jackson's apartment."

"Lord, have mercy, boy! Where do we go? Where do you think she is?" Daria was already rising from the table.

"*We* don't go anywhere. That is the problem with you women," Cole retorted, slamming his napkin down on the table. He told Claire not to get involved. Where in the world was she? Could tap into the GPS in the Denali to find her?

"Daria, I am taking you home. No, actually, we will go to Claire's first. I want to check and see if she made it back there. Maybe she is home. If not, you'll just stay there and wait for her. Maybe she will show up and you can get a hold of me."

Daria's mouth set into a hard line as she leaned on her cane and headed for the door. Cole watched the woman as she quickly moved toward the car.

Throwing cash on the table, Cole hurried after Daria. His mind and heart full of prayer for Claire's safety, wherever she might be. He did not want to live without her.

CHAPTER 18

"Human trafficking follows money. America, being the richest nation in the world, stands to reward human traffickers with some of the highest profits anywhere."

—Nita Belles, *In Our Backyard: Human Trafficking in America and What We Can Do to Stop It*

Disoriented, Claire groggily opened her eyes. Her head ached. She looked around. All she could see was spinning colors. The colors were so vibrant, but the spinning . . . Everything was moving around her all too fast.

Her back felt raw and sore, as if the skin were scraped off. Her shirt felt like it had holes ripped in the back of it. Had she been pulled, dragged across the gravel?

The longer she attempted to focus, the spinning slowly began to stop. Claire looked down and realized her hands were bound together with a tight plastic strip, which served as homemade handcuffs.

Her feet were tied in the same manner, and secured to the bottom of her chair. She looked up into the humid room. It was primarily empty and spacious.

"I must be inside the warehouse." she thought.

She looked over. Her chair was one in a long row of red theater chairs in the center of the room. In front of her was a raised platform of sorts.

"Am I in a theatre?" She wondered. *"What kind of show is this? Everything is so confusing."*

Muted voices and the distant sound of doors slamming made Claire turn her head to search for an escape. The sounds began to stir behind her. She recognized the thud of heavy boots, which made Claire stiffen.

"Who's here?" She called out.

"Hello, Ms. Sullivan."

Claire's thoughts sharpened as adrenaline pumped through her body. She immediately began to classify the voice. Male. Late thirties, at the most. Eastern European accent. Possible smoker. Tall, from where the sound of the voice was coming from.

"Lorenzo Morricone?" she thought to herself.

"So, you and your little friend, Cole Peretti, have been quite the nuisance lately, I see." The voice continued to draw closer until the man sat directly behind Claire. She could hear his pants legs swish as he sat and crossed his legs.

"So, nosy Ms. Sullivan. I thought I would let you in on my little secret. Show you what I have in store for your little pet, Morgan Ann Bishop. Suarez, tell your men to bring them out!" The man ordered. There was a loud sizzle and popping sound, then an overhead spotlight began to shine directly on the now visible catwalk. The dazzling lights made Claire's eyes water.

She was still a bit unsure of herself and her surroundings, frustrated that she was unable to move. She struggled against the plastic ties that bound her hands and feet. Then shadows emerged onto the stage in front of her and she immediately stilled.

Black figures, silhouettes, slight, little shadows. All female.

"Who are they?" she thought.

She let out a sickening gasp, as the realization of what she was witnessing blinded her. Claire leaned forward retching dry heaves and starting to cry, the beginnings of an overwhelming panic attack. The tears, vomit, and sweat caused some of her hair stick to her face.

"This must be a dream. A nightmare. Surely, my nightmares have evolved and this just seems real." she thought to herself. *"No, God. No. Please, when I open my eyes, please do not let me see what I thought I just saw,"* she desperately prayed as she tried to get out of the seat.

The plastic tie wraps bit into her skin with each movement. She could smell wretchedness, blood perhaps, from her hands or her back, and the mix of salty tears and bitter vomit.

Still leaning over, Claire opened her eyes and peeked up at the stage. She could still see the silent parade moving forward like broken robots mechanically marching with their skinny, naked legs. A thin material, nothing more than a wisp of lace, covered their most intimate parts.

There was more to this scene. Each girl's head was completely shaved, intriguingly bald. It made them look almost ugly.

Why shave them? To shame them even more? Make them even more vulnerable? What was the purpose of the shame? Surely, this was mind game for Morricone. It was degrading, reinforcing that the girls were nothing but meat to him. Did he tattoo them as well?

Claire refused to accept what she was seeing. Skin and bones, these tiny females could be no older than fifteen years old. They paraded in a submissive line onto the stage. Without an accurate head count, Claire could only guess how many girls had walked in. Eleven? Twelve? All pale, Caucasian, except, for one ebony-skinned, tall girl at the beginning of the line to the far left whose hair was beginning to grow back.

Each of the girls held empty stares. It was as if their vacant minds were a thousand miles away from the immediate circumstances.

"Do you enjoy what you see, Ms. Sullivan?" The man's creepy tone sent chills up Claire's spine.

Claire shook her head, anger welling up inside of her. What kind of game was this madman playing?

"The buyers will arrive soon. The investors will take their seats right here where you sit. They have traveled great distances, some from Montréal, Amsterdam, and Colombia. These girls will remove those drapes and be bought. The price on their head is a great one."

Finally getting her wits together, Claire frantically searched each of the young girls' faces. Could Morgan Ann possibly be one of these girls? They all looked alike. Where was she?

As if he could read her thoughts, the man's demonic laughter tickled her neck. "No, Ms. Sullivan, your little pet is not here. She is not ready yet. A fighter that one is. We have quite a bit more breaking-in to do before she will be ready to be sold and make me a profit."

"Let me out of here!" Claire yelled. "Girls, run! Don't let this monster win! Don't let him destroy you!"

"Destroy them? Why, no, Ms. Sullivan! I have only just rebuilt them. Restored them. Reprogrammed them. They belong to me, now."

"UNTIE ME THIS INSTANT! I don't know who you think you are. HELP! Someone, please."

"Ms. Sullivan, stop." Traces of impatience threaded through the Serbian's voice. "I wanted you to be the first to see our new line of American products. All run-aways. All between fourteen and sixteen years old. Do not be in such a hurry to leave. You are in for a treat."

"HELP! HELP! SOMEBODY!" Claire screamed.

"Stop that before I lose my patience with you! I have had these girls for an upward of six weeks to three months, but they are ready to go now. Each of them so hungry for someone to love them, to cherish them, to want them. It was easy, actually."

Strong, black, leather gloved hands grasped Claire's face on either side from behind, and forced her chin upward to look at the girls on the stage.

The man's menacing tone growled in her ear. "I am Lorenzo Morricone. Remember my name. Look at their faces. Memorize every crevice and line. See the colors of their skin. Look at them. They see you. They may have even thought you would be their little superhero, their last chance at survival. You, Ms. Sullivan, are nothing, just as they are nothing. You are a scared little girl, like them. They will never be on American soil again once they leave with the buyers. No one will ever find them."

Claire attempted to twist her face free from Morricone's grasp, but that only made him grab her hair and force her head again to look at the stage.

"Parents will move on, Ms. Sullivan, or die looking for these girls. Whatever they choose to do with their dull, ignorant lives. Eventually, they will close their hearts to the pain; however, you, my lovely Ms. Sullivan, will see these girls faces in your mind for the rest of your pathetic, little life. This is a gift from me to you. You will know exactly what is happening to each of them every day. You will be the heroine who just wasn't strong enough to save them from their destiny. Just a moment too late, as always."

He continued to hold Claire's head in his vice-like grip. She was unable to move, unable to tear her eyes off the girls that stood staring back at her, burning holes into her soul.

"In the midnight hour, you will try to sleep, you will see their faces, and hear their faint screams. There will be nothing you can do about it. They will be gone. They will be used over and over again."

Claire could feel the man's hot breath sputter against her ear with each word he spoke. With a growl, she braced her body, pulling at the ties around her hands and feet, as she tried to bite Morricone's fingers. She would try anything to get away.

Laughing, Morricone released her head and sat back into his chair.

There were plenty enough girls to overtake the crazy maniac. Why didn't they see that? They had strength in their numbers. Claire reasoned.

"Try talking to them, Ms. Sullivan," Morricone teased, nodding toward the girls encouragingly. "They belong completely to me. There is nothing you can say or do that I fear. These girls standing before you are only shells.

"Do you know why I shaved their heads? It has become a trademark of mine. I believe that as their hair grows back, it signifies the makings of a new creature. The hair growth shows the time we have had them, kept them, and trained them. When their hair is completely long again, they will be totally new people, with new memories, and new lives. They will no longer be the young children they were when we first obtained them. My buyers don't mind their lack of hair; they are focused on their bodies. Hair can be replaced with a simple wig."

"I'll buy them, Morricone. Every one of them. Please, please let them go!"

Raucous laughter erupted from the demonic stranger behind her, echoing through the empty warehouse. None of the girls even flinched. It was as if they stood asleep.

"Will you now?"

"Yes, Morricone." Claire's voice cracked with the plea.

"I like it when you say my name. Say it again for me. Oh, and how much would you be willing to pay, Ms. Sullivan?"

Morricone inched close behind Claire. His voice tickled her earlobe once again. "What kind of price tag would you be willing to put on their lives?"

Salty tears choked Claire as a wave of impossible desperation washed over her. She did not know what to say. She did not have the answers to his diabolical questions. "Please," she whispered.

Morricone tasted the word on his tongue like a delicacy. "Ah, Ms. Sullivan. Yes, please beg. I like that too, but begging never works. I can tell you how many times I have heard that word. *Please*. Every time I have added a new product, a new girl to my business, I have heard that word, but I still continue to do what I please."

Standing, Morricone walked around the row of chairs and leaned in close to Claire's face. He was a gorgeously sculpted lean man. Darkly tanned, with a strong bone structure. His black hair gelled into place. As she looked at him, the only other individual that came to Claire's mind was Lucifer, the once beautiful angel of darkness.

Morricone's gaze locked with Claire's. His serpent-green eyes sparkled as he played his mind-game. Claire could smell spicy aftershave oozing from his skin.

"And what then? Would you buy these girls?" His voice was intimately close. "I have already captivated these girls. I will never give them back. Just try to take my girls. You will never have them. And even if you did, who would stop me from finding new girls? You, Ms. Sullivan, wanted to see the underbelly of the beast. Here it is. You started this naive little journey of yours and you have found what you were looking for. Welcome to the entrance of my hell."

Furious, Claire spit into his face and lunged forward as much as she could, attempting to hit him with her forehead. She would use any part of herself as a weapon against this monstrous, demon-possessed, beast of a man.

He pulled back before she hit him, wiping her spit from his cheek.

"What would stop me from, say, finding a little girl named Josie? Josephine sounds so much better. Don't you think so?"

"Don't you dare say her name!"

Then, as if the conversation bored him, Morricone abruptly stood from where he knelt in front of her and turned his suit-clad body away from Claire with dismissal.

With a stern snap of his long fingers, Morricone immediately captured each of the young girls' attention. Their eyes found their creator and followed his every move.

"Go," he commanded. In silent obedience, the girls turned and filed out of the room the same way they came in.

"GIRLS, RUN! RUN FOR IT!" Claire called out one last time.

The teenagers may as well have been deaf for all the attention they paid to Claire's desperate pleas. As soon as the last girl vanished from the room, Morricone was back on his knees in front of Claire. His iron grip on her face violently forcing her eyes to marry his.

"Claire Sullivan, this is your only warning! Lay off. Call off the hounds. I have shown you mercy when I show no mercy. You see the nightmare I can put you in. You cannot begin to imagine how I can make your life a living hell. If you meddle anymore, I swear to you, I will break you. I will do worse to you than what I have done to these ugly, little sticks. Is that understood?"

Standing, Morricone took a few steps back then pulled a knife from his pants pocket.

Fury and unblemished hatred bled from her swollen eyes.

In response, Morricone reeled back his arm and slapped Claire across the mouth as hard as he could.

Claire's head swung wildly to the side and tears welled in her eyes. How in the world did she ever end up in this situation?

Then, in an instant, a stronger force deep inside drowned away her self-pity. Maybe an angel of peace descended into the warehouse to lift her spirit.

Curiously enough, an idea she read about in college came into Claire's mind. *Middle of the night courage.* It was a phrase about facing fear, coined during the Civil War and it perfectly described what Claire felt.

She did not know exactly how, but a sudden determination birthed inside of her, replacing her fear with strength. She quieted and sat up straight.

Breathing heavily and wiping the sweat from his wide forehead, Morricone leaned forward to cut the ties that bound Claire's wrists. He had no regard for Claire's skin and whether he sliced through it or not. Then he began to work on the ties around her ankles.

Claire recoiled as he touched her skin. She wanted to kick him, but she was well aware of the knife he held in his hands, and the freedom that was so close.

"My clients will arrive shortly." He pulled a syringe out from his pocket. "You must sleep now." He pierced her skin before she could react.

"When you wake up. The auction will be over. The girls will be gone and you will not be able to report anything to anyone. This, I swear to you, is the only chance you will receive. Pray to your God, or to any god you like, that you never see me again. Because if I see your face again, you will belong to me and I will take you away from everyone you think you love."

Motioning toward the back door with a flick of his head, Morricone restrained himself from the curdling violence that wanted to burst out of him. A bloody mess was not the type of welcome his guests would appreciate. He already had to call one of the girls to come clean up Claire's vomit.

✗

Gradually, Claire began to wake up. She was aware only of darkness, cold concrete, and another debilitating headache.

How long had she been out? Was the auction over? She tried to stand and soon realized she was in a very small space, a closet maybe? She felt the walls and found a doorknob.

She quietly opened the door and peered down a dark hallway. She slowly felt her way down to an unloading area and stumbled down steps that led outside the warehouse. She moved cautiously, in case anyone remained there.

Claire's legs felt on fire as she ran toward the parking lot. Sobbing, she looked for the Denali.

"Cole, oh, Cole! I am so sorry. I need you right now." Claire longed to feel safe in his arms. Cole was so right. She should have never become involved alone.

She spotted her vehicle and ran as fast she could toward the Denali. Tears fell from her face by the time she reached the SUV. The keys were still in the ignition.

She roared the vehicle to life, shifted into drive, and slammed on the gas pedal. Small rocks slung in all directions as she careened through the gravel parking lot toward the open gate.

Her mind kept darting from one loved one to another. She needed to warn Misti, but surely keeping Josie in Galveston was a measure of protection.

What about Daria? Where would she be today? Was she at the church, Nehemiah's Wall, or at home? Daria needed to move in with Claire. The two would be safer together.

And Cole, sweet, wonderful Cole. He was so right, as always. Claire needed him. She should have never tried to find Morgan Ann alone. She should not have taken on the role of a vigilante.

Searching the side door pocket, she found her cell phone. It was dead, the battery depleted. She checked her GPS to figure out where she was, but it looked as if someone had smashed it.

Claire slammed her fist against the steering wheel in frustration. She did not know where to go, or what to do. The web became all too tangled. What a mess she was in.

"Joels!" she thought aloud.

Joels would know what to do. He knew how to get in contact with his partner, Cole. He would be there for Claire. Claire took a deep breath and kept driving. She would keep going until she found a highway she recognized.

She was moving away from the nightmare in the warehouse and, no matter how long it took, eventually she would make it to the precinct. She felt relief as if a weight seemed to lift off her shoulders.

"Please be there, Joels. Please, God, do not let me down now. Please let Joels be there."

CHAPTER 19

"For you will certainly carry out God's purpose, however you act, but it makes a difference to you whether you serve like Judas or like John."

—C.S. Lewis, *The Problem of Pain*

Raindrops splattered down marking the sidewalk as Claire ran inside the police station. She bumped into the police officer who usually sat guard at the end of her street. What was his name? She immediately felt ashamed that she lacked the decency to even know his name. That made her cry even harder.

"What's wrong, Ms. Sullivan?" The tall young man said with alarm. On instinct, he held out his arms and she fell onto his shirt sobbing.

"I don't even know your name," Claire wailed, clutching his uniform. His badge cut into her cheek.

"It's Cruz, ma'am. Miguel Cruz. We've never had a real conversation before, so it's okay. I just know your name because of Peretti. It's okay." He awkwardly patted her back as he tried to guide her into the precinct waiting room.

"And I am Claire. Claire Sullivan, though I want it to be Peretti. Cole and Claire Peretti." That thought made Claire cry even more.

"What's going on?" A thundering voice asked from down the hallway. It was Joels.

"Joels! I have so much to tell you," Claire sobbed, letting go of Office Cruz, much to his relief. She rushed toward Cole's partner.

"Hey! Calm down. Come on in my office and we can talk." She walked in as Joels' held the door open for her. The warm concern in his eyes felt like a safe place for Claire to be.

"Let me start at the beginning," Claire said, sinking into a chair in the corner of the office.

Joels nodded, handing her a box of tissues.

Then Claire began to tell him what happened.

CHAPTER 20

"Hope is the thing with feathers
That perches in the soul
And sings the tune without the words
And never stops at all."

—Emily Dickinson

The text message notification chimed on Cole's phone just as he pulled up to Claire's door to let Daria out.

"The house is dark. No lights." Daria said. She'd hoped to have seen silhouetted movement behind the curtains.

"That means she isn't here for sure." Cole responded grimly as he stared out into the rain soaked streets. Hope slipped away like the rainwater down the street's sewer drains. "I wonder how Maesters is taking all that darkness in the apartment."

"I'm sure Claire left at least one light on for him, Cole." Daria muttered. She folded her arms as she stared out into the dreary night. The raindrops beat against Cole's car in a steady drum.

"Just to let you know, young man, I ain't liking the idea of sitting in an empty house just waiting."

Cole ignored her comment, and looked down to his phone, hoping the message was from Claire. He frowned in concentration as he read then reread the short message.

The cards are on the table, Peretti. We have your prize.

Before he could reply with a return message, his phone sounded again with another mysterious note from the number he did not recognize.

Come rescue your nosy princess, Hero.

Then another text message containing the address. It was in the Houston Shipyard and Harbor area.

"Daria, I gotta go. Please, stay here. I need you here. I can't . . ." Cole stopped trying to explain. "Daria, you have no choice! I just got a text and I think someone has Claire!"

Daria's look was withering.

"I don't know where you are going, but you bet your bottom dollar I am going with ya. Step on it, boy! Not just men have Claire, but spirits of evil. I have been praying as we've been on the road and I knew something ain't right. There is something going on that just ain't what it seems. Something is wrong in my spirit. I feel it."

Cole gritted his teeth and shook his head. There was no arguing with the woman. He did not have time to waste trying to get her out of the car. He had to reach out to Joels and make sure he was at the precinct, ready to go with him. Maybe he could leave Daria there.

Chapter 21

"No man can serve two masters:
for either he will hate the one, and love the other;
or else he will hold to the one, and despise the other.
Ye cannot serve God and mammon."

—Matthew 6:24 KJV

Joels' office phone rang just as Claire finished telling him about the girls and how Morricone had threatened her. It was Cole.

"Hey, man. I was just about to call you. Where you at?"

"It's Peretti," Joels mouthed to Claire.

It's Cole! He called. Claire's heart leaped. She wanted to see him. She was tired of all the anguish. She wanted to spend the rest of her life with him. She wanted their relationship to be okay. Surely, he knew that. She would give up anything for him now. Nothing mattered to her more than the relationship she had with God, and the one she had with Cole Peretti.

Joels nodded as concentration created worry lines on his forehead. He nervously tapped a pen against his metal desk as he listened to Cole on the other end of the phone.

Claire waited. Her body had finally stopped shaking. Everything was going to be alright now.

"Claire is here with me," Joels said. "She was with Morricone. Yes, she's fine . . . Fine, I promise. I have her here with me at the precinct . . . No . . . No . . . Don't worry . . . Text me the address and I'll meet you there. I'm leaving now."

Joels stood up from his seat, grabbed his gun holster and strapped it on.

"I have to go with you, Joels!" Claire said, jumping to stand in his way as he started to leave the office.

Joels scowled. "Claire, please. You know you can't go with me. Are you crazy? Stay here. You will be the safest here. I don't want you to get hurt."

Claire relented, nodding and drooping slightly. She would be a useless casualty if something happened. Then a new thought entered her mind. She had learned the power of prayer. She would stay at the office and pray. The angel armies would fight for her. They would go in her place.

Joels' eyes softened and settled on her. His chin seemed to quake as he stared down at her, though he was not an emotional man. It was not like him to express his feelings so vividly on his face.

"I am sorry, Claire. I really am. I am sorry you had to go through what happened today. Please forgive us; we should have kept you safe."

"I am safe, Joels. I'm here now."

"I've got to go, Claire." Joels nudged her out of the way and headed out of the precinct into the dark and rainy night.

Cole made Daria swear on everything that was holy that she would stay in the car once they arrived at the warehouse. Staying put should not be difficult. Both of their apprehension had lightened once they found out Claire was at the station.

Morricone's text was a trap. He wanted Cole to think they had Claire. Joels would be there soon, and together they could trap Morricone and whoever else was involved. Maybe they would be able to find the breaking house. Maybe they could find Morgan Ann. Morricone's power play was exactly the break Cole needed.

Pulling into the gravel parking lot, Cole saw an old white van parked near the barbed wire fence. He checked the block for any other cars. He saw nothing but a few old beat up pieces of rust parked down the street at a junkyard.

"Daria, please just stay in the car. We need you safe and sound. Joels will be here soon. Just keep the cell phone in hand. I am going in to check out the place. If I don't come out in half an hour, call the police. I will need backup."

Daria understood the seriousness of the situation, and nodded her head as she continued to pray.

Checking his gun, Cole opened the car door and eased out. Saying a quick prayer, he headed down the side of the building to the rear entrance. There were no security cameras, no bolts on the doors. Just an old, tin warehouse once used to store machinery. The Houston Harbor was within eyesight, only a few thousand yards away.

Joels would not be too far away now. He would bring backup and be there soon. Cole eased around the corner of the old building. The only sound he heard was from his shoes crunching the gravel beneath his feet.

The clattering of a tire iron broke the silence several yards away from Cole. He pulled his gun and eased down the side of the warehouse, ready for whatever was there.

"Just come on in, Peretti." The tinny mechanical voice came from a hidden speaker. Cole searched for the source of the sound as it continued. "We aren't going to solve anything if you hang around out there all night. Come along now before I have to send someone out to get you."

Cole started to run back around the corner toward the car and Daria, his empty hand reaching for his phone to call for backup.

"I wouldn't do that if I were you. Daria is already in here with us," the voice continued. "You poor Houston cops. I can't blame you really. You're uneducated. Too easy of a target."

A burly skinhead stepped out from a side door of the warehouse. The man had satanic tattoos covering his face and neck, turning him into grotesque monster. He blocked Cole's way as he tried to turn the corner and run.

"Stop! Hands up where I can see them!" Cole yelled, cocking his gun and pointing it at the man's chest. As the giant continued to move toward him, Cole fired several rounds into the man's chest. But the man kept coming, the bullets trapped in Kevlar body armor.

Baring his teeth, the man smashed his fist into Cole's face, toppling him to the ground. Standing back up, Cole tried a double leg take down on the bigger white guy to no avail. The man grabbed Cole and speared him against the warehouse wall, holding him by his throat.

"Come with me little guy, unless you want me to beat you to a bloody pulp," the man grumbled in what sounded like a European accent. "Give me your gun," the man ordered keeping a grip on Cole.

Trying to put up a fight would only gain Cole another punch in the face. Spitting blood, Cole grimaced and conceded. He needed to get inside the warehouse to find Daria.

Tattoo-face cracked his knuckles and nodded toward an open sliding glass door at the back of the warehouse. Four other burly, tattooed men came out of the building, one was Caucasian and the others Mexican.

Cole's eyes widened. It was a set-up. Where was Morricone? Frustrated at his stupidity, Cole squirmed to get away, but the giant kept a hard grip on his shirt as he grabbed Cole's gun.

Cole wanted to kick himself. Where had all his training gone? Why in the world had he been so lost in thought that he allowed himself to be taken? He was in a royal mess if Joels did not show up.

Once inside the warehouse, Cole surveyed the building. There was another door slightly cracked open along the front wall. A Mexican guy came through the door dragging Daria, who was kicking, screaming, and praying the fires of the Lord's judgment down on them all.

Cole's heart sped up. He could never allow them to hurt Daria.

"Hey, I am here! What do you need her for?" Cole yelled at the man who was holding Daria.

The man pushed Cole around a corner and down a hallway that looked like it used to be the administrative offices of the warehouse.

As they rounded the next corner, Cole saw Morricone casually leaning against a hot water tank, smoking a cigarette. He was close to forty years old, shorter than Cole, and leaner.

"Morricone!" Cole said, recognizing the man from photos. "You got me; let Daria go."

Morricone ignored Cole, watching as the Mexican dragged Daria down the hallway. Her cane scraped the floor behind her, and every once and a while she tried to use it to whack her kidnapper in the shins.

Morricone casually flicked a glance in Cole's direction. His eyes lazily grazed over him like a lion who was not interested in catching a lesser prey. Cole did not scare him.

"Patience. Patience. We're just letting all the pieces fall in place, Cole Peretti. You have no idea what is really going on here, do you?" Morricone asked.

Cole recognized a sharp European accent highlighting each word.

"What are you talking about? Where is Claire?" Cole said, bluffing as he tried to buy time.

Morricone laughed, throwing his head back. "You Americans! Always playing the detective. This story is almost wrapped up. I am almost to the end of this exhausting tale. It's a monotonous book that began with Judge Patrick Sullivan years ago."

The Mexican shoved Daria next to Cole. Cole reached to steady her, but one of the other men who had joined the group kicked Cole in his side with a pointed, steel-toed, snake-skin cowboy boot. A cracking sound came from Cole's ribcage, and he doubled over with the pain of the fracture.

Another other man jumped onto Cole's back, beating him with his fists down further onto the floor. Cole struggled to fight as he heard an old familiar voice yell out.

"Enough!" It was Joels, his old friend.

Better late than never," Cole thought cynically. Cole turned his head toward the voice and spit out another mouthful of blood. Joels stood in the doorway, nonchalantly watching Cole and Daria as if he had been there for a while.

The distanced look on Joels' face gave him away. Cole realized his partner was not there to rescue him.

"What is he doing?" Cole thought. The reality of the situation screamed in Cole Peretti's mind, but he did not want to accept the stinging truth.

Surely, Joels had not set his partner up. All of his training, and years of expertise left him as Cole growled, stood to his feet, escaping the Mexicans, and rushed at Joels.

Nothing mattered now. His partner was a traitor. His partner almost got his fiancée killed. His partner was in alliance with human traffickers, this bunch of sick perverted creatures. What kind of demonic man had Joels turned into? Suarez and Morricone were the evil scum they had been searching for so long, and now Joels was one of them!

Cole barely lurched toward Joels when all five coyotes piled on him, and began beating him down again. Morricone and Joels watched from the sideline as Daria screamed, and prayed for help.

"You should not have gotten involved so long ago with the Sullivans, Peretti." Morricone said. "Patrick Sullivan sent some of our best coyotes to the pen for a lifetime, so he had to go. We killed him, Peretti."

Cole's painful breaths consumed him. He could barely hear Morricone talking.

"You would never let it go. You had to keep searching. You just had to keep looking for the traffickers selling girls on the streets. You would not let the murder of Patrick Sullivan rest, so we bought off your partner years ago. Joels here has been our eyes and ears in your office. You are too nosy. It's time to make that entire situation stop, once and for all."

Joels glanced down at Cole Peretti with cold, calculating, eyes. His normally pleasant facial features twisted into a grimace. His conscience burned out long ago. He had no remorse for what was happening to his longtime friend and partner.

Shallow breathing was all Cole could muster. It hurt to even try to speak. He just wanted to close his eyes and go away from the pain, the betrayal, this nightmare. But Daria. Daria was there. She still needed him.

Morricone squatted down beside Cole who struggled to pull himself up onto his knees. Yanking Cole's head back by his hair, Morricone stared into Cole's eyes. The darkness of an evil spirit lurked behind his smile and danced through his voice.

"But it's not over yet," Morricone whispered. "There's something we have to do to complete this story. I need to utterly destroy Patrick Sullivan's family. He tried to take away my business. He took away my best men, and now you have the heat on the rest of the operation.

"I want Patrick Sullivan to watch me from the hell he is burning in as I destroy his daughter. You and this old Cajun hag will work as my bait. Tonight it all ends." Looking toward his skinhead and Mexican allies, Morricone pointed to his two captives.

"Take these two to the dock. We have a gift to send to Ms. Sullivan. We shall see just how benevolent Judge Sullivan's daughter really is. If she accepts our gift, she'll lose one of you."

Cole gathered his remaining strength and tried to run for the warehouse doors. If he could just get to a phone.

"Shoot him down! But leave him alive," Morricone said. Before the commanding words were completely finished, the reverberation of one of the Mexican's guns sounded throughout the warehouse. Cole fell to the ground, his shoulder bloodied.

"Morricone, you ain't getting away with this!" Daria swore over Cole's agonizing groan.

Joels walked over to Cole and grabbed his arms back tightly, showing no mercy toward the injured back shoulder.

"Joels, what you are doing? The police are coming!" Cole cried as the man tied his hands behind his back with a plastic zip tie.

A Mexican picked Daria up and headed out the door. Joels dragged Cole behind them.

"No, Peretti. No, they ain't. No one is coming. It's just us, man. This is the end." Joels' eyes were iced over. There was no sentiment.

"You can't do this, Joels!" Cole cried.

"It is already done. Get him out of here!" Joels said as he shoved Cole forward into the arms of one of the coyotes. With no further explanation, Joels turned to shake hands with Morricone.

CHAPTER 22

"Monsters cannot be announced. One cannot say:
'Here are our monsters,' without immediately turning
the monsters into pets."

—Jacques Derrida

The screaming rain plummeted in heavy sheets against the office window as Claire paced back and forth. She felt as if she had stayed far too long in Joels' office. She had prayed for every thing she could think of, but the anxiety had not left. She felt as if there was nothing left to say. It was time for action.

She tried calling Daria, but there was no answer. Joels should have been with Cole a while ago, but neither of them had called. Without thinking, Claire picked up a stack of papers on Joels desk and began sifting through them. It was not in her nature to plunder through other people's desks, but her nerves were on end.

A pile of pictures slipped from her hands, falling to the floor. Thinking she had come across a case file, Claire set down the papers and began to gather up the pictures. The photos were of girls; each was quite distinctive. There were at least twenty different faces in the pile, but all of them were about the same age, fourteen or fifteen years old.

"These must be missing girls," Claire thought. *"Runaways. Surely all of them were not being trafficking."*

A cold sickness washed through Claire's stomach as she noticed an ebony-skinned girl with almond-shaped eyes. She had seen this girl before in real life; except that now the girl was bald! Morricone had her! Claire scrambled through the photographs once more trying to visualize each girl with no hair.

"No way. Could these possible be the girls I just saw?" Puzzled, Claire desperately tried to tie all the pieces related to the case together. What was the big picture? How was Joels involved? She knew he and Cole had been on the hunt for the human trafficking ring, but what was he doing with all these pictures?

There was something odd about the photographs. They were all taken in front of the same whitewashed cement wall. How would Joels have known about each of these girls? How would he have obtained photos of all the missing girls, all taken with the same background?

A strange doubt began to gnaw at Claire's mind as she gently set down the eerie prints. Whom could she trust now? Claire peeked through the blinds of Joels' office into the bustling station. Busy men and women were talking on the phone, booking criminals, drinking coffee, and typing on computers. How was she going to ever be able to talk to any of the police in this station? How would she know who to trust?

Taking a deep breath, Claire shut her eyes and prayed harder than she had ever prayed before.

"Lord, please do not let me make the wrong choice. Jesus, you carried the weight of the world on your shoulders; carry me through this nightmare. Consume the unjust, Lord. Help the little ones to hold on."

Opening the door, Claire went to look for Officer Cruz. Before she took three steps into the station, her cell phone vibrated. It was a text message from an unfamiliar number containing an address.

> We have a chess game to finish.
> I let you move too quickly, I see.
> I think it is time to meet your Bishop.
> Your Rook and King are soon to be mine.
> Meet us at the Houston Harbor for your last little gift.
> Checkmate, dear Ms. Sullivan.
>
> Morricone

Confusion was Satan's tool. Rook? King? What did that mean? This was a message from Morricone, but what gift did he have? Morgan Ann? Morgan Ann's last name was Bishop. The puzzle pieces seemed to tumble into place.

Surely, Morricone did not have Cole. Sweet Jesus, if Morricone had Cole who else did he have? The rook? Josie? Misti and Josie were still gone away. Claire fought against the overwhelming darkness that threatened to choke her into a panic, fought to keep her legs from collapsing.

Daria. Wonderful Daria. Morricone could not have possibly found her. Why would he want *her*?

Trepidation licked at her soul as Claire tried to casually skirt the desks and head out into the evening. Officer Cruz, who had become accustom to following Claire's every move over the last several weeks, looked up as she began to leave Joels' office.

"Where are you going, Ms. Sullivan?"

"Um, nowhere, Officer Cruz. I-I think I will just head home. I-I'm feeling faint. I think I just need to rest. To sleep." Claire could not seem to make the jumbled words stop as she fought back the dreadful tears threatening to spill from her burning eyes. Her heart was a panicked bird trapped in her chest, fluttering, flitting, trying to escape.

"Let me take you home."

"No! No. I'm good. Really," Claire said a little too forcefully.

The young police officer searched her face for telltale signs of lies, searching for the hidden truth beneath her seemingly calm façade. He hesitantly nodded, indecisive about accepting her answer.

"If I leave now, without him, I have no hope. No one to rescue us all," Claire reasoned with herself.

"But, Officer Cruz, if you would, could you check on Officer Peretti? Find out where Officer Joels went. Send someone out after him. Make sure Officer Peretti is alright."

Frowning, Officer Cruz tilted his head watching her expression. Examining her fidgeting fingers and wary look.

"Where is Officer Peretti?" Officer Cruz asked.

"I-I'm not sure. I know Officer Joels went after him. Something is going on at the Harbor. Maybe it has to do with their case. I-I don't really know, Officer Cruz."

Cruz began to call the attention of the other officers. Salvation was nigh. The Houston Police Department, knights in their armor. Nevertheless, this mess was too big for them to put all of the pieces back together.

Claire shook her head and went out into the night. She needed to make it to the Harbor before everyone else did. She knew her heart was about to break in pieces. There was nothing to do but brace for the inevitable.

CHAPTER 23

"He brought them out of darkness,
the utter darkness, and broke away their chains."

—Psalm 107:14

Claire painstakingly made her way through the traffic headed toward the harbor. Stoplights gleamed like the red eyes of demoniacs as rain and hail pounded the Denali. Though she wanted to push her way quickly on to her mission, a part of her almost welcomed the delay. It was the anticipation of the unknown that bothered her, the future.

"What next?" She took a deep breath and focused her mind. "I can do all things through Christ who strengthens me," she said aloud. "Thank you God for being my strength. I release the power and authority of the Lord to protect from any spirit that would attempt to attack my mind, in the name of Jesus. Lord, you have declared that our weapons are not carnal, but mighty through God to the pulling down of strong holds."

As she prayed, she began to feel a sense of peace. The Lord was her strength. Her faith resounded with the truth: God was going to take care of everything. All things worked together for good. God would fight the battle before her. He would rescue His people. Faith welled within her as she imagined an army of angels standing at attention.

The reality of knowing the police department was on alert and on their way right behind her also empowered her faith to keep moving. Her confidence soared as she pulled into the gravel parking lot bordering the shipyard.

She found a parking space in front of the pier. Leaving the Denali running, Claire slipped out of the SUV. She stuck her hand in her suit coat pocket to make sure she still had her mace. It the only weapon she had; hopefully, she would not need it.

She stepped onto the wooden boardwalk that led past the parking lot out to the Port of Houston, her eyes searching the walkway for familiar faces. At the end of the dock, she saw the silhouettes of three, possibly four, individuals. Were there more?

The rain calmed to a soft sprinkling as she walked. With each step, she prayed that God's warrior angels were by her side.

As she neared the small group of people, she saw Morricone and her nerves once again began to seize. She never wanted to see him again. She remembered his casual stance and predatory eyes. He stood still, severely calculated, with lethally vigilant eyes.

"Welcome, Ms. Sullivan," Morricone called out, his European accent thick and heavy with each sarcastic word. He stretched his arms out wide, inviting her into the circle of people with him.

Daria stood on one side of the monster, and Cole slouched low on the other on the other side with his hands tied behind his back.

What had happened to Cole? Was he bleeding? And Daria! Why was she there? Was she okay? Was anything broken on her?" Claire thought as she scrutinized her loved ones.

"You have your choice, little queen. What is it? You stupid Americans seem to like riddles. How was mine? The Bishop was not my only pawn. How important is your rook, Daria Rainwater?"

Claire could barely breathe. Daria stood erect with no fear in her eyes.

The golden lights on the pier illuminated patches of the walkway. A thin smokestack stretched into the night sky billowing its fury in the distance. The harbor and pier were deserted. The single smokestack was the only witness to the crimes below.

"Do you know anything about chess?" Morricone asked. "It doesn't matter, you have to play by my rules. I have chosen to bring your little pet back into the game. Here's your piece of trash, Morgan

Ann Bishop." He pulled a small girl from behind him and shoved her forward.

She wore a hoodie that hung like a thin curtain around her haunted face. She was bruised, likely the result of beating from the fists of men. Black rings around the hollow of her eyes signified a prolonged lack of sleep.

It was the first time Claire had seen Morgan Ann in person. Lunging forward, Claire grabbed her and hissed, "Go! Go now! Run."

As Claire urgently pushed Morgan Ann behind her, the poor girl began to slowly run down the long pier toward Claire's Denali.

Morricone's provocative, throaty laughter mirrored his sick humor as his eyes followed the escaping girl whose steps faltered as she ran down the pier.

"That was so heroic of you, but we've already broken her spirit. Take her body with you if you want, but her soul is imprisoned. Her legs can run and take her far away, but she will come back. She belongs to me. That lot you saw today in the warehouse brought me quite the pocket change, if you care to know. I'm sure by now they've already received their buyer's mark, a tattoo claiming them forever. One day, Morgan Ann will go through that process."

A car screeched up next to the Denali, causing Morgan Ann to second-guess herself and glance back at Claire.

"Ms. Sullivan!" She yelled. The teen girl's voice was husky and hoarse. "It's Mr. Joels."

A sudden rush of relief flooded Claire's body almost causing her crumble to the pier.

"It is Joels! He did not leave his partner. He is here to save Morgan Ann, Cole, Daria, and me!" Claire thought. *He is not the bad guy after all. He will be able to explain those photographs.*

Claire watched as the giant of a man stepped out of his police car.

Then, suddenly a question entered her mind. *"How does Morgan Ann know Joels?"*

"Joels! My man, join our little party," Morricone called out, his words sailing past Claire's bewilderment.

Cole spit blood from his swollen lips, and looked up as his partner approached.

The expression on Joels' face was one that dated centuries back. One, perhaps, Judas Iscariot wore in the garden as he betrayed Jesus with a kiss.

"Joels! What is he talking about?" Claire demanded, resisting rational reasoning, refusing to put the pieces together.

"Joels is the reason why it took us so long to find the girl." Cole growled through his pain.

Morgan Ann began to shake and cower from her vulnerable spot on the boardwalk, halfway between Claire and Joels, but the tall man passed her by without so much as a glance of acknowledgment.

Claire stared at Joels as he approached. He had been their friend, someone to trust who was always there, but now he had an unfamiliar tight look on his face and a grim scowl on his lips. He didn't even look like the same man.

"Whatcha got, Morricone?" Joels barked.

"Just a little bit of last minute negotiating before the ship sails," Morricone said.

"Joels, surely you cannot be a part of this, young man!" Daria called out. Then, catching Morgan Ann's eye, Daria called out, "Run, girl! Get out of here!"

"Shut up you old hag," Morricone said, grabbing and shaking Daria's frail body.

"Stop! She's an old woman! Leave her be," Claire screamed at Morricone. "Joels, please help us. You still have time," Claire, pleaded, her eyes still on Daria.

"God, help her! She looks like she is about to collapse," Claire prayed in her mind.

Joels did not even bother to respond. He held the look of a man who had no regrets.

With a quick snap of his fingers, Morricone redirected everyone's attention to the two prisoners beside him, Cole's bleeding, slumped body and Daria's angry rigid one.

Claire was not sure Cole was fully conscious anymore. He slumped forward, barely standing.

"So, Ms. Sullivan. Who's it going to be? You decide. Make your choice. Your king, this Houston pig, or your granny here, the rook? You can only save one." Morricone's eyes shifted to look directly into Claire's. "You do not seem to believe me. I want to introduce you to my friend, my little bee, *Pelicia*."

The light on the pier glinted in the shiny metal as Morricone pressed the M70 pistol into Cole's slumped back. Then, grabbing him by his hair, Morricone pulled Cole to stand up straight.

Daria's wild eyes were as fierce as a den of lionesses. *No way will you choose me, Claire*, her eyes snarled.

Claire's heart thudded. *"How can I choose? I can't! Where is Officer Cruz and his team?"*

Cole's shirt drank in the blood from the gunshot wound to his shoulder. His blood dripped down, darkening the wooden planks of the old pier.

"No, please!" Claire begged. Her mind raced, thinking of ways to stall Morricone a bit little longer. Surely, the police team would show up. Surely, someone other than Joels would arrive soon. She could hear sirens in the distance, and held on to hope they were headed their way.

"Cole, please just hold on. Hold on!" Claire demanded as she held back tears of frustrated anger. A silent prayer shouted through her mind.

"Jesus! Jesus, King of the world, save us. Confuse and scatter our enemies and all these that plot to destroy us. Open my eyes, so I will see that there is more power with me than against me."

"You don't have an answer, Ms. Sullivan? Or maybe you want Morricone to make the decision for you," the Serbian gleamed as he referred to himself.

Morricone's sharp eyes swiftly turned from Cole Peretti's crumbling body to the birdlike older woman, Daria.

"You seem to have such a close connection to *Baba*, Grandmother." Morricone said as he traced a long slender finger across the high cheekbones of the Creole woman's face.

"I have a little secret for you, Ms. Sullivan." Morricone said with a smug, self-righteous air that was so thick Claire could almost taste it. "There's really no street price for an old lady in America, or Eastern Europe for that matter."

Turning his gaze back to Claire, Morricone wickedly caressed her figure with his eyes, simultaneously reaching out to push Cole's weak body to the ground.

"Joels! You've got to do something!" Claire screamed, turning to her old friend.

A twinge of guilt must have pierced his heart. Joel's began to justify himself. "I am in too deep with Morricone, especially because of your father . . ."

The truth buzzed through Claire's ears, deafening her. She did not want to believe what she was hearing. Joels? He was one of the pallbearers at her father's funeral. *"God, no, please have mercy on me. I cannot bear this betrayal."*

"Cole opened too many files, pieced together too many facts . . ."

"What makes you think you'll ever be rid of me, Ms. Sullivan?" Morricone interjected. "To do that you'll have to cross over to our side. You will see me in your dreams. I am a part of you now." He grinned as he held up his gun to Daria's temple.

"Besides, if you were wondering, Ms. Sullivan, I am not much a cop killer. That is not my style. Now, judges . . . Ah, yes, judges are fair game. That is one more sin tainting my past. I hope you are good at forgiving. I recall another Sullivan long ago used to talk about forgiveness."

Agonizing rage flooded over Claire. *"Oh, my God! My father. He killed my father! Lord, take vengeance on those spirits that are warring against my mind, heart, and family."*

Suddenly it was all clear. Morricone was never going to let any of them leave here alive. He couldn't. They all knew too much. He was toying with her, a sick game of cat-and-mouse. Claire had to do something or they were all going to die. Daria. Cole. Morgan Ann.

Breathing a prayer, she screamed and threw herself at Morricone with all her might, but the sound of his gun resounded at the same time.

Daria's wide eyes locked with Claire's one last time. She did not even have a chance to blink before the force of the bullet in her forehead sent her sailing off the edge of the pier and into the murky Houston bay.

Though it happened as quickly as a bolt of lightning appears then disappears in the sky, Claire felt as if time stood still. Everything was black and white, surreal. Surely, this was a nightmare and not reality.

From his place on the pier, Cole grabbed at Morricone's ankles with all the strength he could muster, pulling him off balance and to the ground, separating the maniac from his gun which spun across the pier and landed just teetering at the edge of the platform.

Police cars screeched to a stop. The sound of a little girl's cries—Morgan Ann's—broke through the sirens. Chaos reverberated like the aftershocks of an earthquake. Claire could feel the wooden slats of the pier shaking, or maybe it was her legs.

A speedboat pulled up to the dock and Joels jumped in. "Hit it, Suarez!" Joel commanded. As the boat sped away, Joels fired shots toward the pier where Cole and Morricone were still brawling, barely missing Morricone's head.

Thunderous footsteps from a small army of police officers advanced toward the pier. The men were yelling as they barged between Claire and the skirmishing duo on the ground. One of police officers dove into the dark water after Daria.

Too late! Too late! Too late! The gleeful chants of wicked spirits sounded as they danced around the ancient sacred fire of chaos and confusion.

Claire stood at the edge of the pier as Officer Cruz held her back from leaping into the water.

"There you are. I see you. You're okay. We're all okay." Claire thought as she watched Daria's body floating just beneath her.

"She's right there! She's okay. She will make it! She's strong! She can make it!" Claire voiced her hopes.

Silent screams rocked her body as Claire collapsed into Officer Cruz's arms. A strong memory invaded the nightmare on the pier, and stole Claire back to the day her mother passed away.

"Shh. Listen to Ms. Daria," it was as if Daria were there holding her, rocking her, right there on the pier. "Heaven's gates will swing open wide for us all one day. That is a place of no nights. Jesus is the light of that city. No fear, my child. No fear. And one day we'll get to see that place. Won't you like that, Claire? No more shadows. And your mother will be in paradise waiting for you."

Claire's young head bobbed up and down. More than anything, she wanted to see heaven, to see Jesus and her mother. No more night? No more terror? No more shadows hungry for her fear? Yes! She wanted to go to that place.

"Daria! Daria! Please, please, please don't leave me," Claire screamed toward the gloomy water.

The rest of the moments played out like a scene from a movie before her eyes.

Cole on a stretcher.

Morricone in cuffs.

Claire's eyes flittered from Cole, to Morricone, to the water. Gone. Daria was gone.

"Do you see the darkness anymore? Does the light push back the darkness? Are there really no shadows, Daria?"

CHAPTER 24

"Do not hurry as you walk with grief. It does not help the journey.
Walk slowly, pausing often: do not hurry as you walk with grief.
Be not disturbed by memories that come unbidden.
Swiftly forgive, and let Christ speak for you unspoken words.
Unfinished conversations will be resolved in him.
Be not disturbed. Be gentle with the one who walks with grief.
If it is you, be gentle with yourself. Swiftly forgive; walk slowly,
pausing often. Take time, be gentle as you walk with grief."

—Andy Raine

It had been twenty-four hours since Morgan Ann's rescue.
Twenty-four hours since Morricone's arrest.
Twenty-four hours since Joels escaped with Suarez.
Twenty-four hours since Cole's rush to the hospital.
Twenty-four hours since Daria left the world.

Richard called Misti with the news of what happened, and she and Josie drove back from Galveston to pick Claire up at the hospital after she was assessed for injuries. They took her home, prepared to stay a few nights with her if she needed them.

That night, back at home, reality began to settle in Claire's mind. She would never see Daria bustling around her apartment again. Daria would never make her bed, or fix her beignets. She would never hear her sing again, or ask her to turn down her radio preachers.

Bone weary and exhausted, Claire reached to turn off the lamp beside her bed when she noticed a piece of stationary lying on the nightstand. Picking it up, Claire recognized Daria's cursive strokes. It was the lyrics to a song that Daria must have been planning to sing at church with the women's trio.

Daria had scribbled "The Promise, by the Martins" before she hand wrote all of the lyrics. The words read:

I never said that fear wouldn't find you in the night
Or that loneliness was something you'd never have to fight
But I did say I'd be right there by your side
And I did say I'll always help you fight

'Cause you know I made a promise that I intend to keep
My grace will be sufficient in every time of need
And my love will be the anchor that you can hold onto
This is the promise, this is the promise I made to you

I never said that friends would never turn their backs on you
Or that the world around you wouldn't see you as a fool
But I did say like me you'll surely be despised
And I did say my ways confound the wise

I didn't say you'd never taste the bitter kiss of death
Or have to walk through chilly Jordan to enter into rest
But I did say I'd be waiting right on the other side
And I did say I'll dry every tear you cry

'Cause you know I made a promise that I've prepared a place
And some day sooner than you think, you'll see me face to face
And you'll sing with the angels and a countless multitude
This is the promise, this is the promise I've made to you

So just keep on walkin', don't turn to the left or right
And in the midst of darkness, let this be your light
That hell can't separate us and you're gonna make it through
This is the promise, this is the promise I made to you

The big English bulldog, Maesters, came to the side of the bed when he heard Claire crying. Tonight she made an exception and allowed the fat dog onto the bed to lie beside her. She wrapped herself in a fleece blanket and cried into his fur. His warmth kept her company, though she longed for Cole, who was still in the hospital.

An ambulance took him from the pier to the hospital where he went into surgery to salvage his shoulder from the gunshot wound. When the doctors checked him, they discovered a broken rib, and a few other minor scrapes and bruises, but he was going to be fine. Recovery from surgery would take the most time.

Claire began to pray for peace and strength from the Lord. Almost immediately, she could feel His presence in her home. She began to cry in grief as she prayed, trying to emotionally and spiritually release what had happened. She began to speak in her prayer language, a heaven-sent language she had never learned, but that the Holy Spirit of God spoke through her as she prayed from the depths of her soul.

Over the next few minutes, Claire felt God's restoring power. Her worries and the burdensome weight of her loss seemed to lift off of her shoulders. No longer did she have to carry her fear, for she knew the Lord would fight her battles for her. She held on to the promise that he would remove her sorrow and replace it with joy. She closed her eyes and fell into a deep sleep.

The next morning, Claire stood at her living room window with a fleece blanket wrapped around her shoulders. She watched as the fall wind scattered oak leaves down the road.

Misti bustled around in the kitchen, talking in low tones to Josie, as if Claire were sick.

"I'm not sick," Claire thought, *"just numb."* She had not spoken a single word, except to pray, since the police pulled Daria out of the cold Houston waters.

Misti quietly walked up beside her best friend at the window, both staring out into the day.

It was a moment before she began to speak. "Claire, I just received a call from the social worker. Morgan Ann would like to see you before the hospital releases her to go to the private residential treatment center. The center has accepted her and she'll be starting therapy in the next few days. It is a beautiful place for her to heal using Equine therapy. It is the first facility of its kind in the state of Texas."

Morgan Ann's caseworker was with her at the hospital where she stayed under the observation of a psychologist and other medical doctors. It was a miracle Morgan Ann was handling everything as well as she was. After all of the months of torture, she still had enough fight in her to face reality. She told her story to the professionals, and gave a statement to the police.

Claire was lost in emotion.

"I thought closure and peace would come when I knew what happened to my dad," she thought. *"Why does my world feel even more upside down than ever? If Morgan Ann had not have ran away, then maybe Daria would still be here."*

Claire shook her head to clear the bitter thoughts, took a deep breath, and managed to squeak out the word, "No."

Hope drained from Misti's dark eyes, making Claire's heart sink further into despair.

"Claire, I know how terrible it is to be feel the way you feel. The grief is overwhelming. I've been there. It's going to take time to work things out. But you're stronger than I would be facing what you're facing. That little girl needs you right now. And Cole's out of surgery, so you'll be able to see them both."

Josie stood at the entrance of the living room, quietly observing, her hands folded into the pockets of the apron she wore.

Claire knew Misti was right. She knew everyone needed her, and they all loved her, but she did not have any strength to give to anyone, and she did not want to dig deep to find the strength. She wanted everyone to just let her crawl into the hole deep in her heart and leave her alone.

Claire's mind went to Daria. If there was one lesson that feisty woman taught her, it was to always do what is right for your loved ones. If you do right, everything will be right. The people she loved needed her, and she loved them with every ebbing element of her body, even in her weakness.

Wiping away her tears with the edge of the fleece blanket, she nodded her head. She would go. She would step out into the unknown and accept the spiritual strength that lingered from Daria, like the mantle that fell on Elisha from Elijah's ascending chariot.

She would embody the lessons Daria taught her, so that Daria's life would continue. Daria left a legacy in this world, and Claire needed to pass it on. She would become Morgan Ann's Daria, at least for now.

And Cole. She needed to see him, to know he was alive and hers.

Thirty-five minutes later, Claire sat in the passenger seat of the Denali. Richard drove and Misti and Josie rode in the back.

Claire watched as the dreary day flashed by and the city swept past her in shadowy watercolors. It was as if the entire city was in mourning, splashing raindrops and angel tears onto the vehicle.

They arrived at the entrance of Texas Medical Center. Richard parked and walked around to open Claire's door, guiding her out of the SUV.

The wind blew her hair across her face and into her swollen eyes. Everything was felt dead without Daria. Sweet Daria Rainwater. Claire once again stumbled under the weight of the knowledge that Daria was gone. Misti and Josie steadied her on either side.

"We're here with you," Josie said. "We can do this together; let's go inside." Strength flowed from the young girl's voice.

"Okay. I'm ready," she managed to say as they walked through the automatic doors into the hospital lobby. Claire felt unsurmountable strength from the Lord, as a peace that passed all understanding washed over her mind. She felt renewed as they walked toward Morgan Ann's room.

"Be quick to enter the room," a nurse said as she verified their IDs and scribbled down Morgan Ann's room number. "Pesky reporters have been here, trying to sneak their way in and scoop her side of the story."

Morgan Ann began to cry as soon as they walked into her room. The social worker, her name tag read Ms. Carter, was already there.

"Hello, Morgan Ann," Josie said quietly. Misti wrapped an arm around Josie and they stood by the wall, giving Claire room to walk up to the bed.

Claire sat down in the chair next to Morgan Ann's hospital bed, staring at the girl. Morgan Ann looked down at her hands in shame. The teen's fingers were lined with jagged, bitten nails. Her hands and wrists were scarred red from the vicious aggravation of ties over the previous months. Claire's own wrists were still bruised from her time in the warehouse.

Thick, silent pain mingled with loss in the atmosphere of the room. No one said anything. Everything that could have happened already happened. Nothing was left, except for all of the unknown "whys."

The solid facts of the real-life nightmare were all that seemed to matter, and they were unspeakable.

It no longer mattered that Morgan Ann had met a special someone online and thought she was in love. Morgan Ann's human desire for love, affection and acceptance had been viciously torn from her in a demonic vortex that she could not control.

The same dark energy had sucked the life out of Claire by giving her what she always wanted, the knowledge of what happened to her father, and what she never dreamed of, the loss of Daria.

Both Claire and Morgan Ann were aware of their personal miseries. The losses they experienced were more than either could fathom. In the midst of the somber minutes, Daria's strong Louisiana twang sang out clearly through Claire's mind.

"For I know the thoughts and plans that I have for you, says the Lord, thoughts and plans for welfare and peace and not for evil, to give you hope in your final outcome." It was Jeremiah 29:11 from *The Amplified Bible*, Daria's favorite version to read. *"Never pray for an easy life, dear one, but pray for the strength to endure a difficult one."*

Claire reached out to hold Morgan Ann's hand, and began to pray for the young woman, prayers for strength to endure, prayers for healing and restoration, and even prayers for forgiveness.

"Lord, give us strength to endure all of these hardships. I pray for healing and restoration. Please forgive us our trespasses as we forgive those who have harmed us and wronged us," Claire voiced aloud.

Silently, Claire prayed for God to give her the will and strength to forgive Morgan Ann for being a part of the reason Daria was gone. She asked God to forgive her for placing the blame on the young girl's shoulders. It was truly not Morgan Ann's fault Daria was killed.

"One day, oh God, let Morgan Ann come to the place where she can forgive her captors and forget the hellish nightmares she's experienced. I speak peace and life into her spirit right now," Claire continued.

With a deep breath, Claire squeezed the girl's hand, expecting nothing in return. Nothing could make sense of the past.

Claire expected nothing. She did not expect Morgan Ann to share her nightmare tale, or even return the squeeze of her hand; however, Morgan Ann did squeeze back and together the two women, who seemed to have aged a hundred years over night, held hands and stared out the window into the crying sky.

Chapter 25

"The fact that our heart yearns for something Earth can't supply is proof that Heaven must be our home."

—C.S. Lewis

Claire made her way to Room 238.

Cole Peretti's name was typed in bold black ink on a white piece of paper, which was stuffed inside the nameplate on the hospital door. She held a box of hot bagels she had picked up at the hospital's cafeteria thinking Cole would enjoy some comfort food.

She paused, knocking gently to announce her presence, and then opened the door without waiting for a response. Tucking her head in, she peered quietly around the corner. She did not want to wake Cole if he was asleep, or to disturb a discussion if a nurse or doctor were there.

He was awake, though, and alone, sitting up in bed watching the news on the TV.

Claire's heart ached as she noted the swelling of Cole's beaten face. His face was one she memorized; she knew his features almost at well as her own. His face would eventually heal, but his trusting heart was utterly shattered. Is it possible to un-shatter a heart?

She stared at him, waiting until he looked up to see her before she moved forward.

"Claire!" Cole said, his voice full and deep. He acknowledged her, but would not look directly into her eyes. He pushed a button on the remote with his free hand to mute the reporter. The arm on his injured side was hanging in a sling, as he leaned the weight of his body sideways on his good side to keep the pressure off the packed wound in his back shoulder.

"How are you?" Claire asked removing her overcoat. Claire could not catch his eye. He refused to look at her directly.

"I'm fine. Just resting. How's Morgan Ann?" Cole asked.

"She's fine. Misti and Josie are with her right now. Misti told me you were out of surgery. I needed to see you. I brought some bagels, thought you might be hungry." She paused, leaning in. "Cole?" She whispered, gently touching his face.

At her touch, Cole finally turned to look into her eyes. She saw pain that was deeper than the physical trauma. It was pain like she had never seen in his eyes before, a deep sorrow. Cole lost Daria too, and he lost his partner, Joels, to betrayal. Not only that, Claire had disrespected his wishes and put herself and all of them into more danger than necessary.

How could one man handle such loss, betrayal, and rejection?

A soft answer bloomed into her heart. *I was betrayed. I was rejected. Speak life into this man. Speak peace into his Spirit.*

"Cole, the Lord knows your pain. He was betrayed as well. He knows your heartache. You can still trust in Him. You can stand strong and have assurance that the Lord is on your side. You do not have to walk this road alone. He is here with you. And I am here with you. I love you."

Nodding his head, Cole pressed his face into Claire's hand and started sobbing. It was as if a dam broke inside of him and all of the pressure was released. Answers to questions he refused to ask had been given.

"Thank you, babe. Thank you so much. I was so afraid I was going to lose you, or that I was going to die."

"Cole, I am so sorry. You were right. I will never run blindly into another situation like that again. I promise, I will listen to you! Please forgive me."

"I already have, Claire. You were all I could think about as they were beating me. I was so scared I would never see you again. I love you."

"Cole, please don't let me stay on the sidelines anymore. Marry me. I need you. We need each other."

A big smile crossed his face at her proposal. Laughter shined through his tears and Cole nodded. "Absolutely, Claire. I want you to be my wife. I cannot live another year without you next to me every day. You complete me. God is going to take care of us now. I love you, Claire."

The two kissed, lost in the moment. They were alive and together. Nothing else mattered. They pushed aside all the struggles they were facing in their lives, the funeral they had to plan, and the spiritual battles they would have to fight later when they went back to work in the city.

For now, they simply took solace in one another.

Chapter 26

"Amidst the dark abyss of abuse and exploitation, we have discovered and encountered a God of emancipation and salvation. Everything you want is on the other side of fear."

—Jack Canfield

Morgan Ann had a suite at the recovery center that had a window seat that overlooked a grassy hill where horses grazed. She sat in the cushioned windowsill staring at horses.

Claire stood in the doorway watching her, looking for any sign of emotion on her face. She seemed to be a million miles away. Cautiously, Claire quietly tapped on the door pane.

One would have assumed a bomb had gone off by the way, Morgan Ann jumped and grabbed her arms, fear clawing its way into her eyes once again, a tell-tale sign of Post-Traumatic Stress.

"Shh, honey, its okay. It is just me, Claire. Claire Sullivan. Remember I came to see you at the hospital last week?"

Claire placed a glass vase of peonies on the table beside the bed. "Did you see the flowers?" Claire asked, her tone even and soft as she pointed to the pretty pink flowers.

Morgan Ann's cold stare hardly softened, but she slightly nodded as her eyes fixed on the bright spot of color.

"May I sit down?"

Another small nod.

Claire looked around the square room. The walls were a warm coral hue. There was a rocking chair with a comforting hand-made patchwork quilt draped over it in the corner. Claire gently scooted the rocking chair closer to the girl in the window.

Where should she start? The psychologist, social worker, and grief therapist all had given her conflicting tips on talking to Morgan Ann. *Don't talk until she is ready. Talk to warm her up to you. Just watch the horses with her and hold her hand. Don't touch her; she doesn't need to be touched.*

Cole was the only one who had suggested she pray. She did not touch Morgan Ann, but she did not remain silent. She just did what felt right. Claire bowed her head and prayed aloud.

"Lord, thank You for keeping us through the last few days. Thank You for Your hand of protection. Thank You for choosing to give us a way of escape. Thank You for keeping Your hand of protection over Morgan Ann.

"Through Your sure mercies, You brought Morgan Ann back to us. Please forgive us from our doubts and fears. Let Your grace flow and heal. We need You more than ever now. Be with us, heal our hearts, bind up our wounds. Thank You Jesus. I believe in You. I believe in You."

The sweet presence of the Lord entered the room. It was almost as if a band of angels lined the recovery center bedroom keeping out any spirit of fear or worry that would wreak havoc. It was a time of beauty emerging from ashes, a time of conquering cruelty, a new age of renewed sanity and repressing injustice. It was like a new birth. Morgan Ann was alive and starting over.

The girl stared intently at Claire, listening to her as she prayed.

Claire gently smiled at the young girl; she could not imagine what the teen had gone through.

"Do you want to talk?" Claire asked softly.

Morgan Ann tugged her sweater closer to her and closed her eyes. Claire waited. After a long while, Morgan Ann began to tell her tale.

"It was rainin' when the kidnappers took me. I ran away from home about a week before that. Everything happened so quickly. I met this guy online, a site called Backpage. He offered me a job. We had been talking for months on snapchat before I left. I thought I was in love, but now I know I was just using Jackson to get away from my problems.

"Everything felt like it happened years ago. I have been gone so long. I stayed with Jackson. I guess you met him. He promised he would help me get the job I found on Backpage.

"He introduced me to this guy whose name was Alfonso, a Mexican dude, super hot. I wanted to dance. He said he could help me get started. I wanted to get my driver's license, work, and go do my thing. Alfonso got me a fake ID made, but he kept it. I never did drive.

"I did not know it then, but the best place I ever had was with my foster family, that last one anyways. I have lived with so many.

"I got at a job dancing at Adolf's Lair. It was a weird name for a club, but I didn't mind. The girls were cool or whatever. I met a young girl everyone called Emma. She told me her name was Rose and that she was from Seattle. One night, we were about to go dance and our boss, an old fat lady, came and got us and made us go out back. There was a car waiting for us.

"I got nervous and Emma Rose, that's what I started callin' her, started cryin' and tryin' to run away. Our boss lady hit her over the head with a pitcher we pour beer in. Then she picked her up and put her in the backseat of the car. I didn't have a chance to run.

"Mr. Joels and a Mexican man grabbed me and put me in the backseat with Emma Rose. I will never forget hearing Mr. Joels tell them to go quick. He said there was going to be a raid on Adolf's Lair soon. It confused me until I realized what was happening. The girls working there were mostly all underage.

"There were rooms in the back for customers, but I never worked there. At that time, I didn't know that Jackson had sold me to Adolf's Lair for drugs. All I remember is the rain. I wasn't wearin' a jacket and it was cold outside. They drove for miles and miles with us on the floorboard of the car, with our heads covered in burlap. It was hard to see and breathe from the smell.

"We stopped and they uncovered us. We were on a deserted block. All the houses were old and boarded up. Emma Rose and I was forced into small cement cells in a house on that street. I could never take you to it. I could never explain where it was or even if it was in Houston. I ain't got no idea.

"I was in a small room with just a mattress on the floor. A flickering light bulb hung out of my reach on the ceiling. Nothing happened for the longest time. I was just there in that room alone.

"I was more afraid of the waiting I think. It could have been hours or days; I don't know how long I was there before I began to hear Emma Rose screaming and crying in another room down the hallway. She cried and cried. I heard slaps, and cussing, and other sounds through the walls."

Morgan Ann closed her eyes and covered her ears as if she could still hear the awful noises. It was hard for the girl to catch her breath as the anxiety of her hellish nightmare's memories overcame her.

"Hispanic men opened my door one day, maybe two days or a week later, I can't remember. One grabbed me, yanked me onto the mattress, tore my clothes, and yelled bad names at me. The man laid down on top of me and it hurt. Then he got up and the other man jumped on me so hard I couldn't breathe. It felt like he was almost smothering me.

"After a while, when they were done, a girl named Natalya came in and picked me up off the dirty mattress. I could barely walk, I was so cold, and there was blood.

"The next thing I remember, I was lying between two other girls, Emma Rose and some new girl. I was still in the old house, but I do not know where. I stayed there a long time. There were no windows. We got food, sandwiches and chips.

"A man came in speaking a different language. The other girls tried to attack him so he'd leave, but he beat her. Two other men came in the room. They made us all stand, and strip naked. They looked us over like we were something they were going to buy. I guess that was true.

"The girl that attacked the man was the only one they took. Emma Rose and I stayed. Later, I realized that they bought that girl. I never even learned her name.

"It must have been later that day that I was tied up and they took me to a new place away from Emma Rose. I hadn't met Morricone yet, but that day I did. When I met him, he told me how he had gotten someone to pay off Jackson and that no one was looking for me anymore.

"He said I had no hope of leaving. He told me I was his property now, then he put me in the back of a white van.

"The place he took me was horrible, hell on earth. They called it the 'breaking house.' There were so many other girls there. They shaved my head that first day. I thought that would be the end of my life, or the beginning of hell, whichever. I knew if they ever took me out, if I was ever sold, that the buyers would brand me with a tattoo. I didn't want that to happen, so I kept fighting them.

"I stayed at the breaking house forever it seemed. The days and night mixed together. I thought that was what the rest of my life was going to be like. I wanted to die. I could barely hold on to my sanity, but I never gave in. I never forgot my name. I prayed, hard, that someone out there would not forget me."

Claire felt now was the time she could reached out to touch the young girl. She gently smoothed Morgan Ann's growing hair down, murmuring soothing sounds as the girl cried into a pillow. The girl was safe now, but she had a long journey ahead of her.

"I never even knew what happened to Emma Rose." Morgan Ann cried, shaking her head. "I was so confused the day Morricone dragged me out of the breaking house, and threw me in the white van and took me out onto the pier. I thought he was going to put me on a boat, or drown me.

"I thought someone had bought me and I was going to be sent out. With all my heart, I fought to remember my name, who I was, and where I was from. I could not lose my identity."

Morgan Ann began to rock back and forth as she wrapped her skinny arms around her slender frame. Closing her eyes, she seemed to be remembering more she needed to tell.

"Suarez's men used to put an old dirty sneaker on my face. I was on the floor and they would step on my face. They said I was worth nothing, less than nothing, and that the breaking house was one place I could not run away from.

"They tried so hard to break me, to make me believe that I had no value. The only step left was to sell me and brand me. If they tattooed me, if that ever happened, when that happened, I would be a goner. I would completely lose myself. Every day I prayed that day would not be the day I was sold, and sent away forever."

Claire gently squeezed Morgan Ann's arm.

"You're lucky. You escaped . . ."

Morgan Ann opened her eyes and jerked her face toward Claire. "I ain't lucky," she interrupted. "You do not know how much I prayed. I prayed that God would wake someone up and tell them about me. Please not to let me be forgotten. I swore I'd do anything God wanted. I said I would never run away. I would never make myself throw up again. I would help my foster parents with the younger kids, if God would just please send someone to me."

Claire sighed deeply as she contemplated the horror story. It lined up with her dreams. All of those nightmares she had were an answer to Morgan Ann's prayers. The dreams were God's way of having *someone somewhere* not forget about Morgan Ann. Claire could not speak; it was all too overwhelming.

But now what were they supposed to do? Daria would have known what to do. Daria would have had all the right words to say. How do you eradicate a nightmare from someone's memory? You can pull them from danger and make sure they are safe, but how do you help them forget what they already saw, heard, and experienced?

Suddenly, she had an idea. She pulled a small journal and a pen from her purse.

"Morgan Ann, I am going to give you this journal and a pen. There should be a Bible in the nightstand by your bed. I want you to read the Bible and find verses that bring you comfort. Then write down those verses and how they make you feel.

"Every time you feel overwhelmed, or when you need to talk, or need to try to express yourself, begin to write. The journal belongs to you only. You don't have to share it with anyone unless you want to.

"I will come visit you again next week. I want you to try to work with the staff and try the therapies they teach you. Go to the groups. They can help you. You can trust them."

Morgan Ann nodded and took the journal from Claire. It was a step in the right direction. Squeezing the young girl's arm, Claire stood to leave.

"You promise to come back? You promise to visit me again?" Morgan Ann asked.

Claire smiled, "Of course."

Morgan Ann tried to smile back, then picked up the pen and smoothed down the first page of the journal.

CHAPTER 27

"Sometimes callings from God unfold in an instant but more
often callings happen within a million slow moments."

—Lysa TerKeurst

The testimony of Daria's life made an impact on the community
around her. The sheer number of people at her funeral spoke
volumes to Claire as she peeked around Cole's shoulder into the
overflowing Pasadena church. It was standing room only as the
ushers began to escort Daria's family and loved ones to be seated on
the front pews of the church.

A gorgeous cascade of red roses splayed across the elegant, ivory
casket. Daria's very best friends, Nina and Tina Nobles and Shana
Keni, were all dressed in black, quietly standing on the platform
ready to sing.

Pastor Manguia stood behind the pulpit and looked out into the
crowd. Removing his glasses, he reached for his notes, then paused.

"I came prepared to read Sister Daria Rainwater's eulogy. My
heart is so heavy today, but I know with assurance that Sister
Rainwater is in a better place, dancing on streets of gold.

"I see a room full of people today, which means she touched
people's lives in an extraordinary way. To truly impact a life, one
must truly love others. Daria loved people.

"She was a woman who overcame obstacles by tackling them
through faith, instead of tiptoeing around them in fear. I believe we
can keep Daria's spirit alive in all of us by passing on her memories,
her stories, and her love.

"She will live on if we pick up where she left off, and carry a
torch of determination to see the power of Jesus shine into the

darkest of nights. Daria had a heart to see human trafficking snuffed out, not only in our area, but also all over the world. She died warring against that very evil, and she prevailed."

Claire could see heads nodding in agreement throughout the room as Pastor Manguia continued to speak. Misti, Richard, and Josie sat on Claire's other side, all holding hands as they wept softly.

"Even in the midst of her untimely passing, her life was about setting other people free! An abducted teenager was let go!" Pastor Manguia exclaimed. "This happened because a community rallied around saving that child. People like Daria Rainwater were concerned about human trafficking and refused to give up. Can you picture that type of victory happening for the 30 million people who are trafficked around the world? I can see that happening! We have the power to bring them freedom. You have the power to restore life and help rescue others, just like the young lady from our community was helped."

Pastor Manguia stepped down off the platform to stand beside Daria's casket.

"At the end of every day, as she rested from her labors at Nehemiah's Wall, or after she had spent hours at the church downtown, I am sure Daria asked herself, 'Have I made the Lord and my church family proud? Did I make this world at least a little bit better?' Ever a caring, faithful woman and friend. That was the way that Daria Rainwater lived her life.

"I believe each of us have that same responsibility extended to us. We are to do the same from here on out. I will leave you with these last words before her friends begin to sing. The dream Daria had to open a safe place to help the women on the streets comes true this weekend. The shelter, Nehemiah's Wall, will be dedicated in her honor. Daria would love you all to be there as her dream comes to life.

"Behind every successful woman is a tribe of women who have her back and these women you are seeing here on the platform were exactly that to Sister Daria Rainwater. They will march on with the dream of Nehemiah's Wall in honor of Sister Rainwater. May a piece of her live on inside of each of us."

The women began to sing. It was the song Daria had handwritten and left on Claire's nightstand. After the song, Claire and Cole stood with Daria's family and walked to the front of the church near the casket. People began to stand and say their final goodbyes through the progression line, walking past the casket, and giving their condolences to the family.

Claire felt a soft tug on her sleeve. "Claire?" It was Josie's soft voice.

"What is it, Josie?"

"I went to visit Morgan Ann and she was askin' about you."

"Yes? I saw her a few days ago and will go again next week."

"She wrote a poem, we wrote it together, for Daria. Do you think they would allow her to read that at the dedication of Nehemiah's Wall?"

Claire's smile radiated through her tears. It was a healing moment. The hand of God was working in and through young teens' lives. The recovery center was helping her to heal and forgive.

"Absolutely, Morgan Ann can read y'all's poem. I will make sure of it!"

Closing her eyes and reaching for Cole's hand, Claire lifted a silent prayer to God in thanksgiving. The pain of losing Daria would never go away, but these small miracles in Morgan Ann's life were a memorial to Daria's prayers.

Chapter 28

"Listen to the mustn'ts, child. Listen to the don'ts.
Listen to the shouldn'ts, the impossibles, the won'ts.
Listen to the never haves, then listen close to me . . .
Anything can happen, child. Anything can be."

—Shel Silverstein

The weekend after Daria's funeral dawned bright and beautiful. Claire's morning went by too quickly as she raced down the highway to meet her friends at Nehemiah's Wall. The plan was to meet early to give Morgan Ann a chance to rehearse her poem.

The volunteers from the shelter were expecting a large turnout, including the police department and the mayor's staff. What an exciting day it would be, seeing the beginning of Daria's dreams come into fruition.

Pulling into the gravel driveway, Claire could see the welcome party waiting for her. There was a group of high school kids with red markers drawing bright red X's on each person's hand as they entered the building. Morgan Ann and Josie were both dressed in bright colors, and waved to her from the doorway. Their hands were already marked with a red X.

"Hey y'all," Claire called out as she helped Maesters from the backseat to the ground. They walked up to the girls "What's with the red X's?" Claire asked Misti.

"The girls saw it online. It's the *End It Movement*, which is basically a coalition of organizations that want to draw attention to the human trafficking issue. The red X is a great conversation starter. It's becoming popular, and lot of people are starting to learn what it means."

"Really cool! Give me an X, girls," Claire said. She held out her hand as Josie and Morgan Ann popped the lids off of their markers. Once they finished, Josie smiled and gave Claire a hug. "Come on! Let's go inside. We can't wait for you to hear Morgan Ann's poem!" Josie started skipping toward the door, her long curls bouncing.

"Okay! Okay! Let me put Maesters in the office and I will meet you in a minute." Claire said, laughing as she watched the girls having such a great time.

Claire locked the dog in the office and followed Misti to the prayer room where the ceremony would take place. Shana Keni was adjusting the microphone for Morgan Ann when they walked into the dimly lit room.

"This is the prayer room that will be available throughout the week," Shana explained. "Anyone who wants to come and pray for their city can come here. Today, we will turn the overhead lights on for the ceremony, but normally the prayer room has low lights and gentle worship music in the background."

"I love way this room is large enough to seat a hundred people, but still feels small enough to be an intimate place to pray," Claire said.

"Yes, Daria would come here and pray every day. She loved it. But she also had that practical side to her that saw options in how to use the space," Shana Keni said.

"Y'all sit so Morgan Ann can practice," Josie squealed, clapping her hands.

Morgan Ann nervously smiled as she stood behind the microphone and adjusted her paper on the small podium. She looked so much better and confident already. The bruising on her face had already disappeared, though it would still be many months before the bruising on her heart and mind faded.

Faith welled in Claire's heart. She knew God was in the restoring business and would turn Morgan Ann's life into a victorious testimony.

Morgan Ann's soft voice wavered as she began to read. "I learned a lot about Bible stories writing this poem with Josie, and from the center at Chapel. We titled our poem, *And They Cried . . .*"

"You go, girly! But speak up!" Cole called out as he stepped through the doorway. The arm on the hurt side was still in a sling. "I can barely hear you."

Claire walked over to Cole and took his free hand, which was also marked with a red X.

Morgan Ann nodded her head. "Okay. Our poem is titled, *And They Cried and Sang a Song of Slavery.*" She paused and smiled briefly before she started reading.

> Over twenty thousand people are trafficked
> in the United States each year,
> But are not identified as victims.
> And they cried and their cry came up to God by reason of
> bondage.
> Your prayer should be, "Lord, where do I fit into this battle?"
> And they cried and God heard their groaning.
> Your prayer should be, "Lord, where do I fit into this world? It's
> too painful, too bizarre, and too shadowed to even see?"
> And they cried and God remembered them.
> Look now, what do you see?
> Remove your shoes of apathy.
> Step now into this modern day Exodus.
> Turn aside to see. What do you see?
> And they cried and God looked upon them.
> Deliverance waits concealed in a burning bush.
> Salvation unconsumed.
> Locked in a moment, in a choice, in a decision.
> And they cried and God appeared in a burning
> experience and saw a man.
> God has seen the sorrow of the oppressed.
> Be the voice for those who have not found their voice.
> Say, "Here am I."
> Let the Salvation of many call unto you.
> Let my people go!
> And they cried and God called and beckoned from the bush.
> Let him send you as he sent Moses of old.

Let my people go!
Leave a legacy in this world.
Sing a new song.
Drown out the old verses of slavery.
Songs like:
Let my people go!
You are worthy
You are strong
You are beautiful
You are loved
You deserve so much better than this
So much more than this
You were born an innocent child
YOU ARE HUMAN
Let my people go!
And they cried a song of slavery.
Rise up! Rise up, now!
Put off your sandals of apathy and unawareness.
Let these songs be whispers into the ears of our youth as they too
begin to light a fire and define their future with their voices.
Let my people go!
And they cried and God sent forth a deliverer.
Let my people go!
Be that deliverer."

The room was silent as Morgan Ann concluded her poem. Claire was in awe of the power of Morgan Ann's words. She felt the presence of God in the room.

Shana Keni was the first to reach out to give Morgan Ann a hug. The whole room seemed to grow brighter as Josie followed suit.

Claire beamed through her tears as she watched her best friends embrace Josie and Morgan Ann.

Today was another positive step in the right direction, not only for Morgan Ann's life, but also for the life of so many other girls and women in the Houston area that Nehemiah's Wall would reach, touch, and save.

Cole squeezed Claire's hand, then let it go and wrapped his arm around her shoulder. "How is my fiancée?" He flirted, kissing her cheek. "You know, a girl can't be a fiancée without a proper proposal to prove it."

Claire's eyes widened. With everything that had happened, she had not even thought of her impromptu proposal at the hospital or their engagement being official.

"This time, I'm doing the asking," Cole said with a wink as he eased down on one knee, careful for his shoulder.

"Claire Sullivan, will you do me the honor of being my wife? Will you be Mrs. Peretti?"

"Yes! Yes! Of course." Claire smiled, bending down to kiss Cole. She held out her hands to help him up off his knee.

"That's better!" he said with determination as he wrapped his good arm around her.

They stood together watching as more of the staff, volunteers, and community members started pouring through the door for the dedication ceremony.

Before them stood a great wall of opposition called human trafficking, but by God's grace, through prayer, awareness, and intervention, chains would be broken and slaves set free. Lives would be transformed and restored, and love would live on through each of them. Prayer warriors would begin to pray unified prayers of faith.

An adventure was on the horizon. An adventure filled with hope, fear, danger, and deliverance. It was time to continue pushing back the darkness; this time stronger than ever before.

Finally, my brethren, be strong in the Lord,
and in the power of his might.
Put on the whole armour of God,
that ye may be able to stand
against the wiles of the devil.
For we wrestle not against flesh and blood,
but against principalities, against powers,
against the rulers of the darkness of this world,
against spiritual wickedness in high places.
Wherefore take unto you the whole armour of God,
that ye may be able to withstand in the evil day,
and having done all, to stand.
Stand therefore, having your loins girt about with truth,
and having on the breastplate of righteousness;
And your feet shod with the preparation
of the gospel of peace;
Above all, taking the shield of faith,
wherewith ye shall be able to quench
all the fiery darts of the wicked.
And take the helmet of salvation,
and the sword of the Spirit,
which is the word of God:
Praying always with all prayer
and supplication in the Spirit,
and watching thereunto with all perseverance
and supplication for all saints;
And for me, that utterance may be given unto me,
that I may open my mouth boldly,
to make known the mystery of the gospel,
For which I am an ambassador in bonds:
that therein I may speak boldly, as I ought to speak.

—Ephesians 6

Acknowledgments

First and foremost, I want to thank the One true Lord Jesus Christ. May He reign forever as the eternal King of my heart. Without Him, I am nothing. Without Him, I can do nothing. I long to serve Him all the days of my life. May this book outlive me and stretch on into the future to touch lives and further the Kingdom of God.

To my husband, Craig Jesse Aranda. Thank you for being my very best friend, my Godsend. You are the one who knows me inside and out, better than any other person alive. Thank you for believing in me. Thank you for being my rock and my safe place. Thank you for loving me and always shouldering the burden without complaint. Thank you for making my life easier. I love you now and always, Gargs.

And to my children. I wrote this book thinking of you and the impact you will make in the world.

**Like arrows in the hand of a warrior
are the children of one's youth.**

Caelyn, not born of my body, but placed in my life and born in my heart. I pray blessings over you. I pray God guides your footsteps and you learn to acknowledge His voice in your life. God can mightily use you to reach a lost and dying world.

Magalena, you are my crowning jewel. You are so beautiful. I am so proud of you. I pray you stay sweet and kind-hearted all the days of your life. Go, explore, travel, do, and be. Never place limitations on who you are, or what you can discover. Always allow God to use your hands and your feet in His Kingdom.

To my baby that was never born. You, my precious little love, are with Jesus. The heroine of the story holds your name, **Claire**. I smile when I think of you, yet I hold tears in my eyes as I miss you. How can I miss someone I never met? You are an additional reason why I long to go to Heaven one day. I hold no evidence or proof that it is possible, but I like to believe it was you who whispered in God's ear in my darkest hour and helped send me a miracle to alleviate the pain of a broken heart.

Ruben Gary, my firstborn son. My fierce, wild boy. I love you more than you can imagine. I pray God uses your voice to reach the nations. Be fearless and bold all the days of your life. Refuse to be weak. Be strong in the Lord and in the power of His might. You are a mighty arrow that we shoot into the future.

Jonathan Aylan, my little sunshine. My miracle. My unexpected gift. You bring joy to all those who know you and meet you. There is not a day that goes by that I do not thank God for you. Everyone falls in love with you just as hard and fast as I have. You are a gift from God for all of us. Thank you for coming into my life and making it a better place.

Guide their footsteps, Lord. Never let them stray. Keep them safe. Protect their heart always.

Mom. Nonna Doll, I love you. Thank you for your strength. I want to be strong like you are, and I want to always make you proud. From your #1 girl!

Dad. Thank you for instilling in me a love for the Word of God and for Truth. Thank you for unknowingly giving me memories of seeing you sit on the couch reading your Bible before you would go to work in the morning. Thank you. One day, I want to hear my children say they saw me read the Bible and it made them want to know who God was for themselves.

Lynsey, my baby sister. You are the one who can make me laugh like no other. I'm glad we are sisters. I never want to lose you. I will always be here for you. NLYPSFY

M.C. and S.D. You know who you are. You are two of my very best friends in all the world. As you read this book, you will find scatterings of each of you throughout the pages, an author's nod to your friendship. I love you now and always. You were the ones to help me pray when I did not know how. Let us go to Heaven together.

Riq, Issa, Roman, Vanna, Jessie, Sam, Harry, and Ana. Thank you to all of you, my opinionated friends with whom I have spent long hours in emotional and loud debates. You are my treasured friends God placed in my life.

Ms. Vickie Poole, my fifth grade teacher. She saw something in me I only dreamed would happen. While others were catching up on schoolwork, she let me doodle stories in my notebook. She believed in me. She knew I had a book inside of me that the world needed to read. This book is for you, Ms. Poole. It is well overdue. Thank you for believing in me as a little girl. For years, I have held on to your question, "Have you written that book yet?" I can now finally say, "Yes! Yes, I have." Please enjoy. I have thought of you every step of the way.

David Lisenby, Bailey, Fayth McCoy and Elizabeth Hughes. Thank you for the photo shoot. That day in Orange, Texas was so much fun. Though we had only just met each other, it felt so normal to talk and laugh with each of you as we acted out the scenes for the cover design of this book.

David Lisenby, you are an amazing photographer. Thank you for your keen eye.

Fayth McCoy, you are one of the most gentle, beautiful, godly women I have ever met. Thank you for playing the part of Claire. You have such a sweet spirit.

Rachael Hartman, Editor and Publisher, Our Written Lives. You are a pleasure to work with. You have made this road so easy. Your optimistic outlook blew every doubtful cloud from my sky. You made my book possible.

Without you, I would still be holding the skeleton of a book in my hands spouting gibberish about how I was going to write a book one day. You have become a friend.

Thank you for never scoffing at any idea I had, but always taking my words and gently maneuvering them into somehow making sense. I pray God always blesses your business and life.

SWLA Abolitionists

Hi, my name is Rusty Havens. I'm the founder of Southwest Louisiana (SWLA) Abolitionists and a volunteer with International Justice Mission (IJM). SWLA Abolitionists is an NGO that works to end human trafficking both locally and globally through raising awareness, offering prevention training, advocating for better laws, working with law enforcement to ensure rescues.

We partner with individuals and community organizations to help restore every survivor we come across. IJM is the world's largest anti-slavery organization that works to protect the poor through 17 field offices all around the world. So far, IJM has rescued over 25,000 people from oppression.

Human trafficking is very real in SWLA and in cities all across the globe. My organization, SWLA Abolitionists, has helped women who were sold out of downtown bars, inside casinos (often with employees' help), in local hotel rooms, and on our street corners. Every single day, there are 25-45 new ads for women and children in the Lake Charles area listed on a website known for human trafficking.

Human trafficking isn't just sex trafficking, it's also labor trafficking. We've received reports of local labor trafficking in cleaning services, magazine sales crews, and construction crews. There was a large national case that happened close by in Breaux Bridge.

A seafood plant was caught locking people up, forcing them to work 18 hour shifts, and threatening them with shovels if they complained or asked for breaks. Thankfully, the company was caught and order to pay over $250,000 in back pay and fines.

I've seen the darkness of human trafficking as I read online message boards for buyers, and through monitoring local trafficking hot-spots.

How has society come to this? Isaiah 59 says God saw that there was no one to intervene to help the oppressed. Human trafficking continues because of our lack of knowledge and our apathy to act. It's time for us to learn, stand up together, and make a difference.

One person or one group can't end human trafficking alone. It will take all of us coming together to push back the darkness. To do nothing isn't an option; we have to join the battle. And the good news is, the darkness is losing. I've seen what comes from people standing up and doing what they can to help. God uses it and blesses their willingness.

Through prayer, phone calls, and petitions, laws are enacted to better help survivors and make harsher punishments for traffickers.

Through sharing about human trafficking with friends and family, we can recognize victims and save them.

Through monthly recurring donations, SWLA Abolitionists provides a local hotline for area victims to get help. We also have a website where people can read local news stories about trafficking and learn what they can do to help.

Through members of our community connecting and getting involved, aftercare services such as counseling, medical exams, tattoo removal, and shelters are available to survivors.

I've seen the light while visiting with a local survivor who is a mom raising her own family. I've seen it while playing musical chairs with child survivors in the Dominican Republic. The light beaming from the mom's eyes and the Dominican children's smiles will always be with me. It is beautiful. It is worth fighting for, even loosing yourself for.

I, recently, heard the Ryan Stevenson quote, "If you have no interest in invading the darkness, it was useless to give you a light." It's time to shine our light into the darkness and rescue the oppressed until everyone is free.

Please visit www.SWLAAbolitionists.com and www.IJM.org to learn how you can help.

Author's Note

Human Trafficking is part of a dark and painfully sinister side of society that most choose not to acknowledge. Writing this book has been a journey of facing harsh realities, and devastation of lives around me. I have felt heartache and cried along the way. This story has always been a part of me, and now has finally birthed.

Though *Pushing Back the Darkness* is fictitious, there are moments of truth laced throughout. The idea began as a vision over fifteen years ago. One night in prayer, I had a clear vision of a young girl screaming, alone in a bedroom looking out a dark window.. My vision became Claire's dream in the book. I always felt as if I would meet the girl in my vision one day, but in reality it was the seed planted in my heart to write this book.

At the time of my vision, I was attending Michael Shane Brandon's sessions concerning Apostolic Authority. Brother Brandon was infused with the wisdom of the Lord. He taught us about prayer, spiritual warfare, and the power of the Holy Ghost, which gave us the ability to bind strongholds in the spirit.

The Lord began to lay writing *Pushing Back the Darkness* very heavily on my heart. This book is the fruit of many years of prayer and growth. I have pushed away the incredible feat of writing more than once, but when I began to "pray circles" (read *The Circle Maker*, by Mark Batterson) around my book and ask God to breathe fresh life into it, I began to see changes.

There was a particular soundtrack I put on repeat and listened to almost every time I sat down to write, *Nefarious: Merchant of Souls*. The lyrics were somewhat of a muse for me.

I realized God loves authors. He is an author! God was transforming me through the writing, as the author and finisher of my faith. Completing *Pushing Back the Darkness* was not just about finishing a manuscript and seeing it published. It was about God molding me into the vessel He wanted me to become. I was like the clay on the Potter's wheel, where lumps of self-will, doubt, and many other things, needed to be worked out of me.

God had to put pressure on me and allow me to experience utter chaos in my life before I was able to open my eyes and see real heartache in the world. My prayer is that I continue to be a willing vessel God can use to impact the world.

My Passion

Over the past five years, I have met people in various organizations that have utterly changed my life and the way I see people. My burden for the poor and needy of our nation has tremendously increased. Jesus said we would always have poor people around us, and that when we minister to them, it is as if we are ministering to Jesus Himself. If anyone longs to know the heartbeat of God, begin to care for the poor and needy.

In November of 2014, my husband, oldest daughter, and I were a part of a large organized outreach effort in New Orleans, Louisiana. That weekend trip literally changed my life. I will never be the same again.

It started early in the morning. We drove downtown looking for homeless people. When we saw someone, we stopped and gave them hot coffee, a scarf and mittens, and started talking to them. When we really connected with a person, we invite them to join us for breakfast. We loaded them up in our cars and took them to a casino buffet where they could eat as much as they wanted.

Later that day, we hosted a huge block party in a city park. There was live music, food, and games. We were able to reach out to neighborhood latchkey kids and gang members alike. Hours before we arrived at the park to setup, there was a shooting. The victim, a football coach, went to the hospital. We were able to minister to the people in the area, help ease their fear, and pray with them. I learned about the heartbeat of God that weekend as we reached out to the lost and underprivileged.

I had to bring my experience back home with me. I could not allow what happened that weekend to die. I wanted to recreate it. I was so excited when my church agreed to organize two mission trips the following year! The first trip was to a homeless shelter for veterans in Vinton, Louisiana.

We arrange a wonderful Valentine's banquet at the veteran's shelter, complete with rib-eye steaks and all the sides. The look on their faces was priceless. Some of them were enjoying the first steak they had in years. Three of the veterans began to ride our church bus to attend services. One man, the shelter's cook, received the Holy Ghost!

When you do something for the Lord, go all out! Do it all the way. Make no exceptions. Make things happen and always keep it classy.

The second mission trip was strictly for women. All of the volunteers went to serve at a battered women's shelter. We filled plastic totes with toiletry items that would fit under these women's bunk beds at the shelter. We collected over fifty name brand purses, which were donated to the women at the shelter. They were able to take their pick. What woman doesn't like a new purse? Then each woman received a gorgeous yellow rose, and we verbalized how they were loved and special.

The Spirit of the Lord was with us as we walked into that women's shelter. Our team sang and preformed a sign-language interpretation. By the end of the day, three women received the Holy Ghost!

There are hungry souls all around us, just waiting for us to make a connection and bring Jesus to them. They may not walk through our church doors, but if we take Jesus to them, they will respond. We must reach our hurting, dying world before it's too late. When you love God, you love people!

In the Bible, when Nehemiah heard of the ruined condition of the city of Jerusalem, he wept, mourned, fasted, and prayed. His heart was broken because his city was vulnerable, open to devastation, and experiencing destruction. That is how I feel when I see brokenness in the lives of people. When I see people bound by sin, and living life unloved, it breaks my heart. That's when I pursue God's heart and seek out how He can use me to help rebuild and encourage the lost and discouraged. I pray that God would keep me sensitive, and I pray God's heartbeat would become my heartbeat.

Houston

My husband is a crane operator and travels extensively. One month in late 2014, he was working in the La Porte, Texas area. We decided I would meet him and take a trip driving through Houston. There was a bookstore he wanted to take me to.

As we drove along the interstate, we flashed by a sign on a plain brown building. The only part of the sign I could read at the speed we were going was the word "Elijah." I felt the tug of the Lord leading me to investigate further. I had to know what that sign said and what that building was. I *needed* to know.

I think I scared my husband because I yelled for him to turn around! We eventually exited through the traffic, and turned around to scope out the building and the sign.

That day was a turning point in my book-writing journey. Up until this point, I laid my dreams down about writing a book. I thought I would continue in local mission work, helping people in need around me . . . Until that day when I came face to face with *Elijah's Rising.*

At one point in time, that brown building was a brothel. Now, it was a beacon of hope for the city of Houston. Their website states the following about their mission:

Elijah Rising is ending human trafficking by equipping a new breed of justice warrior for prayer, awareness, and intervention in the spirit of Isaiah 1:17.

Elijah Rising is part of a citywide, city-owned justice prayer movement, built on an apostolic-prophetic foundation, with an eye toward a night and day, musician-led expression of victory over sex trafficking. The movement is rooted in the worth of Jesus

Christ and is operating with a growing understanding that we are in the end-times battle described in the Book of Revelation. Since their beginning in 2010 as a once-a-month prayer meeting, they have become increasingly convinced that unless angels and demons move on the issue of sex trafficking, all of our human efforts will be futile. We cover several hours weekly of joyful, musician-led prayer for the ending of slavery in our city. We also raise awareness and conduct interventions that increase points of initial contact with women and children who are caught in the jaws of the commercial sex trade in Houston.

Elijah's Rising is located in Galleria West, one of the most sexualized districts of Houston. Their headquarters building now stands as a beacon of light. Located at 5818 Southwest Freeway, the building once housed an Asian brothel called Angela Day Spa.

Elijah's Rising offers a one hour educational tour to educate people on the dangers of human trafficking. They teach people what to look for to identify areas of human trafficking. Many brothels pose as massage parlors and other established places of business. The tour drives past various locations known to be dealing with human trafficking exploitation.

Angela Day Spa was an original stop on the tour, and *Elijah's Rising* had followed its activities for many years. After a dispute with the property owner in 2013, to their astonishment and through a set of divine circumstances, *Elijah's Rising* was given the opportunity to purchase the building they had been praying over for years!

They signed a lease on the property and watched as the traffickers were evicted. Only the Lord can flip immorality into redemption. Their headquarters, which once housed sexual exploitation and every kind of degradation, now stands as a testimony of God's faithfulness to those who cry out for justice day and night.

I learned so much on the *Elijah's Rising* van tour and through their museum. I have visited the ministry multiple times, and took my daughter on the tour. I believe it is our duty to educate the next generation to make lasting change in the world. It is our responsibility to future generations. Someone once said, "Man is born free, but everywhere he is in chains."

Get Involved!

What can you do to help? The simplest thing you can do is save the following numbers in your cell phone. **1-888-373-7888** is the National Human Trafficking Hotline. **233-733** is their textline. If you suspect that you see or hear of something that may be human trafficking, contact them ASAP.

I sincerely pray that *Pushing Back the Darkness* affects and changes each reader's heart. I pray with all my heart that readers begin to involve their churches, communities, and cities to end human trafficking.

If we all join forces, we can alleviate human trafficking. I believe it is far past time for Christians throughout America to open our eyes to what is going on around us. It's time to move, pray, and become involved in ending human trafficking.

Allow the Lord to take you on a journey as He did me. I am still learning and growing, but I am awake to truth, and I realize my role and responsibility now. I am to pray, write, speak, educate, and push back the darkness!

LAURA ARANDA

LauraAranda@OWLofHope.com
www.AuthorLauraAranda.com

Our Written Lives
book publishing services
www.OurWrittenLives.com
OWL of Hope, LLC

CPSIA information can be obtained
at www.ICGtesting.com
Printed in the USA
LVOW13s1939210717
542174LV00004B/8/P